PART ONE

DISCARD

1

My friends and I did a horrible thing.

We murdered Candy Shutt, a girl in our class, and then we ran away.

Well, we didn't exactly murder her. It was kind of an accident. But we caused it. We sneaked into her house. We tried to steal a piece of her jewelry. She came after us. She grabbed for it.

We watched her tumble down the stairs. We heard the horrible *crack* her neck made when her head hit the wall. We saw her body sprawled at the bottom of the stairs, so still . . . so unnaturally still . . . her head tilted at such a wrong angle.

We knew Candy was dead. And we ran.

We didn't tell anyone we were there that

night. We kept our secret. Just the three of us—Nikki, Shark, and me.

That was in October. And now it's a month later, and we can't stop thinking about it. Dreaming about it. Talking about it.

Some nights I dream of Candy's big silver pendant with the glowing blue jewels. She called it an *amulet*. I see Candy wearing it, using its evil, casting spells on me and my friends.

And then suddenly, I'm wearing the amulet. And in the dream, I feel all strange, as if I'm outside my body, watching myself, falling into the blue glow of the jewels, surrounded by blue, changing . . . changing into some kind of evil creature . . . changing into some kind of roaring beast. A roaring beast in a tight blue shirt. I'm practically bursting from the shirt. I see red lettering on the front. And I know it's blood. Words scrawled on the shirt in blood. I struggle to read them as the blood pours down the front of the shirt.

And suddenly I can read it clearly. My name?

NATE GARVIN, YOU MURDERED ME!

And I wake up screaming.

Yes, it's happened two or three times. And I have to make up an excuse to my mom, who comes running into my room, her face wide with alarm.

"Nate, why are you screaming in your sleep again?"

I blink my eyes. I can't make the blue glow fade away. It lingers like a fog in front of me. "Uh . . . just a bad dream, I guess. I was dreaming about school."

That's what I tell her.

But of course I was dreaming about Candy. Poor, dead Candy, who fell down the stairs right in front of us. Crack . . . crack . . . *crack*. And that amulet, which we all believed to be so evil.

It's hard to understand if you don't live in Shadyside. If you grew up in Shadyside, you'd know all the stories about the Fear family. They were early settlers of the town. They built a huge mansion on the street named after them—Fear Street.

People claim they were evil. The Fears used the dark arts and evil sorcery to get their way— and to entertain themselves. Weird howls and screams of horror were heard coming from the

Fear Mansion day and night. When we were kids, most of us were too frightened to put a foot anywhere near that street.

We even learned about the Fear family in school.

Simon and Angelica Fear were the most evil of them all. Angelica wore a jeweled amulet that she said gave her immortality. She used it to cast spells and put curses on her enemies.

I never believed any of the stories. I don't believe in evil curses or casting spells on people. I always thought the stories about the Fear family were made up.

But when Candy Shutt showed up wearing a silver amulet with blue jewels, bad things started happening to me and my friends.

I know it sounds crazy. But we became convinced she had found Angelica Fear's amulet. And that she was using it against us.

So we sneaked into her house and tried to steal it.

And that's when the accident happened. That's when Candy fell to her death.

We were left standing there holding her amulet. The evil amulet. *Only, it was plastic and glass.*

Yes, a total fake.

Not Angelica Fear's amulet. A cheap copy. With no magical powers. A cheap copy that broke in half, just the way Candy broke.

Candy died for nothing.

Nikki, Shark, and I ran from the house and never told anyone.

But it's a month later, and I wake up screaming.

I know it wasn't my fault. But how can I make the nightmares stop?

2

Some nights it helps to go hang out and talk with my friends. We wait till our parents are asleep. Then we sneak out of our houses and head for Nights, the all-night bar on Fear Street.

We call ourselves the Night People.

I don't know who started it. Maybe Jamie Richards and Lewis Baransky. But now, a whole bunch of us Shadyside High kids sneak out nearly every night.

After midnight in Shadyside, the houses are dark and silent. The streets are empty. Hardly anything moves. The whole world belongs to us.

No one knows about our secret life except Ryland O'Connor, the bartender at Nights. Our parents think we're snug and sound asleep in our beds.

We usually start out at Nights. Then we

wander around town. We don't do much, just hang out. You know. Enjoy the darkness and be together in our secret world.

And now here it is, a cold November night, a tiny crescent moon high in the sky, and I creep out the back door of my house, eager to see my friends.

The wind is blowing the trees, making them shake and rattle. They are dark, trembling shapes behind a curtain of fog.

I have had the nightmare again. This time, a girl was wearing the pendant. I couldn't see her face, but I could hear her whispered words: *"Kill again . . . kill again!"*

I don't think I screamed. But I woke up in a cold sweat. Stood up in a blue haze, as if the pendant were in the room, the glowing blue light floating all around me.

"Kill again!"

So unfair. I didn't kill anyone. Why can't I lose the frightening dreams?

I trot down the driveway to the street, squinting into the low swirls of fog. And I feel the fog inside and out, as if I'm part of it. Not real at all. But smoke floating through smoke.

Whoa. Nate, get a grip, dude.

Don't totally lose it now.

I lower my head and jog a couple of blocks. Nights Bar is just a few blocks farther. No people in sight, but everything is in motion. The wind bends the grass and sends pebbles dancing along the street.

The fog grows thicker as I turn the corner. I slow to a walk, breathing hard. My breath fogs up in front of me. Fog everywhere.

Candy Shutt's house is on the next block.

I stop. A chill shakes my body. I don't want to go past her house tonight.

The nightmare repeats in my mind, playing out in the fog. I see Candy's dead body, eyes staring blankly up at me.

Why me?

I spin around and start in the other direction. I'll walk through the woods, I decide.

The Fear Street Woods.

The bar is on the other side of the trees, on Fear Street. Actually, Nights stands on the very spot where the Fear Mansion stood.

They tore down the mansion last year. It was a burned-out wreck, anyway. They tore down all the old houses on Fear Street and built a shopping center: Fear Street Acres.

So the street isn't scary anymore. It's filled with cars and bikes and shoppers all day. The Curse of Fear Street is over. At least, that's what they said on all the TV news shows.

I wish I could believe it.

A wall of fog rises up in front of the trees. As if trying to keep me from entering the woods. The trees are old and tangled and tilting one way and the other. But their leaves have fallen, and I can see lights on the other side. The lights of the shopping center.

My shoes crunch on the frosty ground. Dead leaves crackle as I walk along a twisting path. The trees rattle and sigh. I hear an animal scamper through the low shrubs at my right.

I'm about halfway through the stretch of trees. The woods are narrow here. Wisps of fog float in front of me. I trip over a fallen branch and stagger forward to catch my balance.

I brush away a clump of tall reeds and start to walk again. The path has disappeared, but I can see the lights glowing hazily beyond the trees.

I start to walk faster—then I stop. I stop when I hear the hoarse *caw* of a bird. High over my head.

I stop. Another chill tightens the back of my neck.

Everyone knows *there are no birds* in the Fear Street Woods.

That's one of the mysteries of the place.

I raise my eyes to the dark, shivering tree branches. I squint from tree to tree. No sign of it.

Another *caw*—raspy, angry.

And then I see it. A huge blackbird, hunched on a low branch right over my head.

Pale moonlight ripples down through the fog. The light appears to burn the fog away. And, suddenly, I can see the bird clearly.

Its long wings are tucked back, so it appears to be wearing a black cape. I see its long talons curled around the branch. I see its curled bill.

It stares at me with a bright, blue eye. Then the bird tilts its head, and I see the other eye. Black? No. An empty socket. Just a dark hole where the eye should be.

I take a stumbling step back.

Why does it stare at me so intently?

We have a short staring match. The blue eye peering down at me, locked on my eyes.

And then the ugly, one-eyed bird raises its head. It lets out a terrifying cry—a high scream that echoes off the bare trees.

Before I can move, it dives off the branch and swoops down at me, pointed talons raised to attack, screeching in fury.

3

The big blackbird lands heavily. I let out a startled cry as its talons dig into the shoulders of my coat.

It beats its heavy wings against my face. It opens its bill in another screech.

I stumble back against a tree. I raise both hands to protect myself.

Its talons dig deeper into my shoulders. I feel the sharp point of its bill scrape the side of my face. The wings pound harder.

I swing my arms. Grab frantically at its fat body. My hands slide off the coarse feathers.

"Owww!" I scream in pain as the bird lowers its bill to my face. Pecks at my eyes.

I twist my head away. Shoving it. Pushing at it.

The wings flap and scrape my face. The

ugly bird grips me tightly, holding on so it can attack. Again. Again.

I feel hot blood pouring down my cheeks.

"Get off! Get OFF!" I scream.

I stare into the empty eye socket. I can see torn veins and muscles deep inside, as if the eye had been *ripped* out of its head.

Another shrill screech of attack rings in my ears.

I feel dizzy.

This isn't happening. This *can't* be happening.

No way I'm being attacked by a one-eyed bird in the middle of the night in the Fear Street Woods.

But it *is* happening.

And I can't fight the bird off. Too strong. Too heavy and strong.

And angry.

I bat at the bird with both hands. Swing at it, twisting my body, ducking my head.

It scrapes my face again. I feel its sharp bill dig into my skin. Blood pours down both cheeks, from my forehead, over my eyes.

Can't see.

Can't see through the flowing blood.

I drop to the ground beneath the beating wings.

I drop to my knees and struggle to cover my head.

But I feel the pinch of pain as it digs its talons into the back of my neck.

It attacks again. Again.

I'm whimpering now. Covering my head with both hands.

Helpless as it lowers its head to attack again.

"Get off! Get OFF!"

Helpless.

Is it going to kill me?

4

How long was I in the woods? What happened to me there? Why do I have streaks of caked blood on my jacket?

I can't answer those questions.

I feel dazed and shaken. And every part of my body hurts. But I can't answer any questions.

I pull open the door of Nights Bar and smell that familiar beery aroma. I blink a few times, letting my eyes adjust to the low lights.

I squint at the yellow neon Budweiser sign behind the long bar at the front. It says: one-thirty.

I step up to the bar and call to the bartender, Ryland O'Connor, who doesn't pick up his head from the *Biker* magazine he is reading.

Ryland is a tall, stocky, red-faced guy, with spiky blond hair, a silver ring in one ear, and crinkled-up eyes that always seem to be laughing. He has three tiny, blue stars tattooed on his right temple. And a long scar on one cheek that he won't tell anyone how he got.

"Hey, Ry," I say, my voice hoarse. "I really need a beer."

He slowly gazes up at me. "Aren't you forgetting something?"

I blink. "Oh, yeah. For sure."

I back up and kiss the brass plaque on the wall by the front door.

The plaque shows the two original Fears— Angelica and Simon—just their faces, young faces, like they're in their twenties or maybe thirties. Underneath, it says, FIRST SETTLERS OF SHADYSIDE. FEAR MANSION BUILT ON THIS SPOT IN 1889.

We all kiss the plaque when we come into Nights. I mean, just about everyone kisses it. Partly as a joke, and maybe some of us think it keeps bad luck away. I'm not so sure. My friend Galen kissed it one night and his lips got stuck to it. It was horrible. He wound up in the hospital. The weird thing is it happened right after

he told me he knew something really important about the Fears. Something dangerous!
But I kiss it, anyway.

Ryland slides a bottle of Bud across the bar
to me. He knows none of us Night People are
old enough. He knows we all have fake IDs.
But he's cool about it.

I tilt the bottle to my mouth and take a long
pull. My neck aches. All of my muscles ache, as
if I've been in an accident or something.

I turn and take a few steps beyond the bar.
I see my buddy Shark sitting with Lewis
Baransky in a booth against the back wall.

"Hey, Nate—" Jamie Richards calls to me.
She's at a table with Ada, my girlfriend. It
seems weird to call Ada that. We've only been
going out a few weeks. It just sort of happened. I'm not really sure how.

We've been friends for a long time. And
then, suddenly . . . wow.

I walk over to Jamie and Ada. I lean down
and kiss Ada on the lips. She raises her hands to
my face—then jerks them away.

She stares at me wide-eyed. "Nate—what
happened to you?"

"Huh? What do you mean?"

Both girls are staring at me now. I drop down in the chair next to Ada.

"Your face——," Ada says. "Is that blood?"

I raise a hand to my cheek. It feels crusty. It hurts when I touch it.

Ada reaches her hand into my hair. "Oh, gross." She makes a disgusted face. "Dried blood. In your hair."

Jamie frowns at me. "What happened? Are you okay? Were you in an accident?"

I shut my eyes to think about it. I have a hollow feeling in my stomach. And my brain . . . my mind is a blank.

"You're totally scratched up, Nate," Ada says, grabbing my hand. "Look. There's blood on your hands, too."

"Hey, Nate—you get in a fight?" Shark calls from the back. "Who won?"

"Definitely not me," I shout back.

But I don't feel like joking around. My ears are ringing. I take another long pull on the beer bottle.

Ada and Jamie are still staring at me. Ada brushes some caked blood off my hair.

"I walked here," I say, thinking hard. "Through Fear Woods. I . . . uh . . . think I fell."

"Did you land on your head?" Shark calls.

Lewis laughs. He has a high whinny of a laugh. He sounds like a horse.

I make a fist. "I'm going to land on *your* head!" I tell Shark.

Shark jumps to his feet. He sneers at me like he's tough or something. "Dude, you want to take it outside?"

I jump to my feet.

Everyone laughs. They know Shark and I are good buddies. Shark is a pretty wild kid. He gets in trouble sometimes. But he'd never fight me. We look out for each other.

Especially since that night at Candy's house. Especially since we have that big, awful secret to keep.

Ada pulls me back down. "So you were walking here and you fell?"

I nod. "Yeah. I guess I cut myself on some brambles."

She shakes her head. "Must be really tough brambles," she mutters. "You're a total mess."

Ada pulls me up and leads me by the hand to the bathroom at the back of the bar. It's a filthy mess. The sink is rusted brown, and there are clumps of wet toilet paper all over the floor.

"Doesn't Ryland ever clean this place?" Ada asks.

I shrug. "He's got a tough job. You know. Sitting up front and reading magazines all night."

Ada wets some paper towels and starts to mop the dried blood off my face. It really hurts, but I don't flinch or anything. Gotta be tough, right?

She frowns at me as she dabs at my cheek. "You sure you fell?"

I hesitate. I almost tell her the truth. That I don't remember how it happened.

But that's just too weird. When I think about how my mind is blank, I get that scared, hollow feeling in my stomach again.

"Yeah. Fell," I said. "Stupid, huh?"

"Yeah," she agrees. "Stupid."

We kiss for a while. I put my arms around her and hold her tight. I want to hold on to her for a long time. Something scary happened to me in the woods, and I don't know what it was.

I only know I'm really afraid.

After a long while, Ada pulls away from me. We're both breathing hard. I can still taste her lips on my lips.

"Let's get out of here," she says, pressing her forehead against mine. "It reeks."

When we return to the table, Shark and Lewis have joined us. Lewis is holding hands with Jamie. They've been going out for years. Shark is spinning a large gold coin around on the table.

"Is that real gold?" Jamie asks. "Where'd you get it?"

Shark holds the coin up for her to see. "It's very old. Know where I got it? That night we were all in the Fear Mansion last year. In that hidden room we found. Before they tore the house down. That night we swiped all that stuff?"

Jamie took the coin and examined it, turning it over. "I'll bet it's real gold."

Shark grinned at her. "Maybe I'm filthy rich and don't know it. I took a whole pile of these coins from that room."

Jamie spins it on the table. Shark grabs it up. He finishes his beer and walks over to Ryland to get another one.

Lewis is wearing his down parka, even though it's about eighty degrees in the bar. He turns to me. "You look tense, Nate."

I don't answer. I don't know what to say to that.

"We're all tense," Ada says. "Everyone at school is tense. Haven't you noticed?"

I tilt the beer bottle to my mouth. "Because of Candy?"

Ada nods. "A lot of people think it wasn't an accident. They think Candy was murdered."

Whoa. I nearly drop the bottle. Shark and I were there. We *know* what happened. We *saw* Candy go flying headfirst down the stairs, screaming to her death.

Shark glances at me. He tucks the gold coin into his jeans pocket. "People think there is a killer out there?"

Ada narrows her eyes at him. "They say it wasn't a human killer. They say it was the curse of Fear Street."

I shake my head. "That's so over," I say. "Fear Street is a shopping center now. How can anyone still believe that stuff?"

Shark taps the table. "We're sitting right where the Fear Mansion stood." He shouts to Ryland behind the bar. "Hey, Ry—think this bar is haunted?"

"Yeah. By you guys." Ryland doesn't lift his head from his magazine.

"Hey, you love us," Shark replies. "If we didn't come here every night, what would you do?"

Ryland grins. "Enjoy the peace and quiet?"

The front door swings open. We all turn. A girl steps into the neon red light at the entrance.

The red light shimmers and wraps around her like a cloak.

And behind the curtain of red, I see . . . I see another figure. A dark figure rising above the girl.

I lean over the table and squint into the eerie light. It's a bird. A giant blackbird. It raises its wings and beats them hard, as if fighting off the red light.

I see one blue eye. The eye seems to be staring into the bar, staring straight at *me*!

I know it.

I recognize that bird from somewhere.

And I open my mouth in a scream I can't stop.

5

Ada jumps up. She shakes me by the shoulders. "Nate—what's wrong? What *is* it?"

The girl takes a few steps into the bar. Behind her, the bird vanishes.

It just disappears into the red neon. The last thing I see is its blue eye.

I take a deep breath and hold it. I watch the girl approach. Did she know that bird was hovering above her? I don't think so.

Ada squeezes my shoulders. "You're trembling," she says. "What made you scream like that?"

Everyone stares at me.

I keep my eyes on the girl. "I . . . I guess I freaked because of that girl," I tell them.

I don't want them to know I'm suddenly seeing strange, one-eyed blackbirds.

"The girl looks so much like Jamie," I say. "I . . . I thought I was seeing double."

Jamie laughs. "Of *course* she looks like me. What's your problem, Nate?" She gives me a gentle shove. "It's my cousin Dana. Remember I told you about her?"

My heart is still pounding.

Up at the front, Ryland is telling Jamie's cousin to kiss the plaque on the wall. She hesitates. She waves at Jamie. Then she leans forward and gives the plaque a peck.

"Remember?" Jamie whispers. "Dana is going to live with me and my family. For the rest of senior year."

I'm starting to feel normal again. But I can't lose the picture of that staring blackbird, floating in the red neon above Dana's head.

"She looks so much like you," I tell Jamie. "Isn't she the one you don't like?"

"Sshhh." Jamie shoves me again. "Here she comes." She turns to the others. "Be nice to her, guys. She's had a horrible year."

Dana steps up to the table. She has Jamie's wavy, black hair and her round, high forehead and dark eyes. When she smiles, she has Jamie's smile.

"Hi, everyone," she says.

"You made it. I didn't know if you were coming or not," Jamie tells her.

Shark pulls over a chair. "I'm Shark," he says. "That's Lewis, and that ugly dude is my friend Nate."

Everyone laughs.

Dana pulls out the chair and starts to sit down.

"Nice to meet you," she says. "I'm Dana Fear."

PART TWO

6

My name is Dana Fear, and I'm seventeen. A week after I moved in with my cousin Jamie Richards, she threw a party to introduce me to her friends. That was very nice of her.

Jamie hasn't always been nice to me.

We didn't get along when we were kids. My first memories are of Jamie pulling my hair and not letting me play with her dolls.

She had shelves and shelves of dolls, I remember. And a big, clean room, with bunk beds so she could have sleepovers. And she had a huge closet filled with toys and games and videos.

My room at home was about the size of her closet. My family was poor, and we lived in a tiny, falling-down house on the edge of the Fear Street Woods.

Jamie's family never visited our house. We always went to her house. Her father was a lawyer or something, and my parents were always talking about how rich they were.

They lived in a big, stone house in North Hills, the fancy part of Shadyside. I remember the long driveway that curved around to the back. They had a barbecue grill with a tall chimney built right into their patio, and their own tennis court.

Funny, the things you remember from your childhood.

I remember standing with Jamie on her tennis court one day. She spilled out a big, wire basket of tennis balls. They rolled all over, and she ordered me to pick them up.

I ran around the court, gathering up tennis balls. And when I filled the basket, she spilled them all out again.

She thought that was a riot. She tossed back her head and laughed. I thought she was really mean.

When I was ten, my family moved away from Shadyside, and I didn't see Jamie for the longest time.

Last year, I heard about her accident. I

didn't know the details. I heard she was at the old Fear Mansion when it was torn down, and she and her friend Lewis fell into the hole for the new foundation. A mountain of dirt started to fall in on them, and they were almost buried alive.

I called Jamie when she finally got home from the hospital. She was surprised to hear from me. She said she couldn't remember the accident at all. She knew that two off-duty cops had rescued her and her friend Lewis.

She said she had a bad hip, which made her limp. But everything else seemed okay. She was totally bummed that she had spent so much time in the hospital in rehab for her leg that she wouldn't be able to graduate with her class. She had to do senior year over again.

We talked on the phone about seeing each other someday, even though we were in different cities. Of course I didn't know then that my life was about to blow up, and that I'd have to come live with Jamie and her parents for the rest of senior year.

Last week, when I climbed the steps of her front porch, I set down my suitcases and my hamster cage, and I took a deep breath before ringing the bell.

I had a heavy feeling in the pit of my stomach.

What would Jamie be like? I wondered. I knew she'd still be pretty, with those big, dark eyes and her creamy, pale skin and wavy, black hair.

But would she be glad to see me? Or would she still treat me as the poor cousin she was forced to hang out with?

I raised my finger to the big, brass doorbell—and the door swung open before I could ring it.

Jamie came rushing out and swept me up in a warm hug. She stepped back to look at me. Then hugged me again.

"You look so fabulous!" she gushed. "I—I can't believe you're here! It's so awesome you're going to be living here!"

She picked up my heaviest bag. "You're tall now," she said. "I was always taller than you, wasn't I? I remember those awful yellow Reeboks you used to wear, without any laces, right? You thought that was cool or something, but it was so geeky."

I laughed. "I didn't think you'd remember me at all."

She narrowed those dark eyes at me. "Of course, I do. I remember everything. I was bossy then, totally mean to you. I guess it was because you were so quiet and sad-looking and ... shy."

"I'm not shy anymore," I said, grinning.

It's true. No one would ever call me shy. For one thing, I'm really into guys. And I know how to get their attention.

I may not be as pretty and dramatic-looking as Jamie. But guys think I'm hot.

I like to go out and party and get trashed and get crazy.

It helps me forget how sick my life is.

Wow. When Jamie greeted me like that— like a long-lost friend—it meant so much to me. I thought I'd burst out crying. I really did.

I need Jamie to be my friend. My life has sucked for so long. I need this new start. New friends. New *everything.*

I picked up the hamster cage and peered inside. Hammy sat in a corner, burrowed down in the wood shavings, staring out at me with those shiny, black eyes.

I knew he was confused, moving to a new home. Well . . . I was confused too. Confused and hurt and angry.

I picked up my other suitcase and waited

for Jamie to lead the way. She wore an oversize, white T-shirt pulled down over black yoga pants. Her hair fell in loose strands around her face, tied in a single ponytail.

Her skin was paler than I remembered. When she smiled at me, I could see tiny, blue veins pulsing in her temples.

She limped badly as she led the way to the front stairs. I realized she was still not fully recovered from her accident.

I wanted to ask her a million questions about it. What were she and Lewis doing at the wreck of the Fear Mansion? How could they ever fall into such a deep hole? Why were they there so late at night?

The questions could wait. Maybe Jamie didn't even remember the answers.

I followed her up the front stairway. "Dana, you have the whole attic to yourself," she said. "It's very cozy. I think you'll like it. Is that a hamster in there? Better keep him away from my mom. She's allergic to all kinds of animals. What's his name?"

"Hammy," I said. "Clever, huh?"

She laughed. "How did you ever come up with that?"

We were both breathless by the time we dropped the suitcases to the floor in my new attic room. I set the hamster cage down on a table in front of the window. Gazing out, I could see the long, front lawn with its two flower beds, empty now since it was November. Two tall, old trees stood on both sides of the driveway, mostly bare except for a few clumps of dead, brown leaves.

Jamie lifted one of the suitcases onto the narrow bed against the wall. "Sorry about your mom," she said.

"Yeah, sorry," I muttered. "Sorry, sorry, sorry."

She wasn't expecting me to be so bitter. I could see the shock on her face.

"Such a bad year for our family," she said softly. "First, cousin Cindy died, then your mom. How is your dad doing? Your mom died so suddenly. He must still be in shock."

"How should I know?" I asked. My voice trembled. I didn't want it to. I wanted to sound calm and controlled. But sometimes I just can't hold in my anger.

"He won't talk to me," I said. "He can't deal with me, I guess."

Jamie put a hand on my shoulder. "Just because he sent you to live here . . ."

"He didn't *want* me!" I cried. "He didn't want me to live with him. My mom dies. So he sends me off to a cousin I haven't seen in seven years. How should that make me feel? You tell me, Jamie. How should I feel about that?"

I was talking through gritted teeth. I looked down and saw my hands coiled into tight, red fists.

Jamie took a step back. Her face went even paler. I could see she was surprised. She studied me for a long moment.

"Dana, you're scaring me," she said. "I'm serious. You look so angry, like you could kill someone."

Kill someone?

No way. What a strange thing to say.

Did I really look like that?

Kill someone?

Me?

7

It was an excellent party. Jamie had the music cranked up. And the dining room table was loaded down with pepperoni and onion pizzas and long submarine sandwiches.

No beer. Jamie's parents were home. But everyone seemed to be having a good time, anyway.

Danny, Jamie's seven-year-old brother, printed out a banner on his computer: WELCOME, DANA—each letter in a different color. It was strung up over the piano.

Danny is a cool little guy. He has short, blond hair and bright, blue eyes, and a killer smile, even with two front teeth missing. Tonight, he had a fake tattoo of a dragon on one cheek.

Everyone was making a fuss over him. One

of Jamie's friends was trying to teach him how to dance. But he kept stomping down on her feet. He thought that was a riot. Each time he did it, he giggled like a fiend.

The first two guys I bumped into at Jamie's party were Nate and Shark. I'd met them a few nights before at the bar everyone goes to late at night.

Shark told me his real name is Bart Sharkman but everyone calls him Shark. He is a big, athletic-looking guy, kinda intense, nervous. He kept gazing around a lot. I think it was hard for him to stand still for very long.

He is cute. I like his spiky hair. I wondered if maybe I could get the shark to bite. But then this streaky-blond girl named Nikki came over to us and wrapped her arm through Shark's.

Nikki seemed okay. She had a funny sense of humor and a hoarse, smoky voice that I liked.

Nate was kinda cute too. Sort of a cuddly teddy bear type. I knew right away why I could be into him. He reminded me of Dustin, my old boyfriend. No joke. He reminded me of Dustin big-time. So in a way, I kinda felt I already knew Nate.

He had a great laugh. I was teasing him about something and we were having a nice talk. And I guess I had my hand on his shoulder—you know, just being friendly—when this skinny, red-haired girl practically bumps me out of the way.

Jamie hurried over and introduced us. She said the girl's name was Ada Something. I didn't catch the last name. I'd met Ada at the bar the other night, but we didn't get to talk.

Sometimes you get a flash about someone. I mean, I don't really believe in first impressions. But tonight I could see that I probably wasn't going to like this girl Ada.

Just a hunch.

I went to get a Coke from the cooler, and when I turned around, Ada was all over Nate. I mean, I'm not against Public Displays of Affection, but I think she was making a point here, staking out territory, if you know what I mean.

I was just talking to the guy, after all.

I guess maybe I was too intense, standing there staring at them. Because another girl came over and pulled me aside. She was tall and very pretty in a cold sort of way. She had perfect, creamy skin and long, billowy blond hair.

She said her name was Whitney. And she held on to my arm and started talking about Ada and Nate, in a loud whisper. "Ada had a crush on Nate for years," she told me. "But he always looked through her like Saran Wrap or something."

Saran Wrap? *Excuse me?*

"Anyway, after Candy Shutt died, Nate was totally messed up," Whitney continued. "I'm not sure why. I mean, he didn't even *like* Candy. I guess it was the idea of someone we knew, someone in our class dying like that.

"Anyway, Ada tried hard to get him to snap out of it. And they finally started going out."

"And now it's a serious thing?" I said, watching the two of them lip-locked on the couch.

Whitney nodded. Her hair fell over her face, and she brushed it away. "Yeah. Ada is really intense about Nate." She raised her eyes to mine. "I just thought I should warn you. You know."

"Look, I was just talking to him," I said. I don't know why I snapped at her. She just annoyed me. "Are you really trying to tell me I can't talk to some guy without permission? Tell your friend Ada to chill—okay?"

Whitney let go of my arm and stepped back. She couldn't hide her shock from her face. She turned bright red. "I . . . was only trying to help."

"Sorry," I said quickly. "Please. I'm kinda in a haze or something. I didn't mean that. It's been really tough. Losing my mom and . . . having to move to a new place senior year."

Whitney tugged at two long strands of her hair, studying me. I guess she accepted my apology, because she said, "How are you and Jamie related?"

I raised my eyes and saw Jamie across the living room, dancing with little Danny. I had to sigh. Jamie was always so graceful and athletic, and now she had that bad limp. She used a cane around the house but quickly hid it away if anyone came over.

"My mom and Jamie's mom were sisters," I said.

Whitney kept studying me. "So your dad is a Fear?"

I nodded.

"That means Jamie *isn't* a Fear?" Whitney asked.

I laughed. "Are you worried about her? Worried it might be catching or something?"

Whitney blushed again.

Why was I being so nasty? Jamie throws a party for me, and what do I do? Make sure all her friends hate me.

But I knew kids were staring at me because I'm related to the Fear family. I'm not a paranoid nut. I don't think people are staring at me all the time.

But Jamie's friends were definitely checking me out. And not just because of my short skirt and glittery, tight-fitting midriff top.

As the party went on, I overheard kids talking about the Fear family. And the Curse of Fear Street. Sometimes they'd hush up when they saw me come by. Sometimes they kept right on talking.

I carried some paper plates into the kitchen and saw a group of kids huddled around the table. They had tense expressions on their faces, and they were talking about Candy, the girl who had died.

"That jeweled thing she wore. It belonged

to Angelica Fear," said a red-haired girl in a jeans jacket and denim skirt. "It was Angelica's evil amulet. She used it to cast spells on people."

A tall, skinny boy snickered. "How do you know that?"

"Galen saw an old photo," the girl replied. "It showed Angelica Fear wearing the same pendant. Galen started to tell people about it, remember? And he ended up in the hospital."

"So you think the amulet got Candy killed?" another girl asked.

The red-haired girl nodded. "Someone murdered Candy and stole the amulet."

"That's way weird," a boy said. "Everyone knows she fell down the stairs. It was an accident."

"Then explain why the police didn't find the amulet anywhere," the girl replied.

The skinny boy scratched his spiky hair. "So you think there's a killer out there? A killer who has an evil amulet that once belonged to the Fear family?"

The red-haired girl didn't answer the question.

I was standing at the sink, eavesdropping. It

took me a few seconds to realize that she was staring at me. They were all staring at me.

And I knew what they were thinking. I saw the suspicious looks on their faces. And even a little fright.

They knew that I'm a Fear. And they knew I'd been listening to their conversation.

I had hoped for a clean start.

I'd had such a bad year, filled with so much sadness and horror.

I'd hoped to leave it behind.

But the cold looks on their faces made my heart sink.

I turned away and hurried from the kitchen. But the question repeated in my mind:

Am I going to be in trouble because of my name *once again*?

8

I made my way back to the living room. A lot more kids had arrived. Their voices rose up over the booming music. Lots of laughter. Some kids were singing some kind of school song, only with dirty lyrics.

Some guys had sneaked in cans of beer, which they tried to hide at their sides. I heard a loud crash. Shattered glass. Someone yelled, "Oops!"

Jamie bumped into me, carrying a tray of plates and glasses. "I have to order more pizza," she said, shaking her head. "I didn't invite all these kids. I don't even *know* some of them."

I laughed. "I just thought you were majorly popular!"

Jamie hurried away. Someone grabbed my arm. I turned to see Nate smiling at me.

"Come on. Let's go outside," he said, shouting over the voices. "We can't talk in here." He gave me a gentle tug.

I glanced around. "Are you sure Ada won't mind?"

His smile faded. "She doesn't own me."

I followed him out the front door. It was a cold, clear night. A tiny sliver of moon was almost lost in a sky full of stars.

Cars jammed the driveway and both sides of the street. One of them was parked on Jamie's front lawn.

Nate shook his head. "Mr. Richards isn't going to be too happy about that."

I hugged myself, trying to stay warm. My little midriff top wasn't much good against the cold. My arms had goosebumps up and down.

Nate appeared tense. He had his eyes down on his sneakers. "Sorry about Ada," he muttered. "I mean, the way she pulled me away like that."

"No problem," I said. I didn't know *what* to say. "How long have you been together?" I asked.

He shrugged in reply. "I'm not even sure we *are* going together."

"Liar," I said, grinning. "That's not what I heard."

He grinned back.

I guessed he was interested in me. Maybe *very* interested.

I didn't mind. I was interested in him, too. I thought, maybe he'd like to put his arms around me and warm me up.

But he didn't make a move. He just stood there, staring down at the ground. "Hey, maybe you and I could hang out or something," he said finally.

"Cool," I said.

Then he ruined it. He raised his eyes to mine and said, "I've always wanted to meet a Fear."

"Really?" Is that why he's so interested?

"I have a lot of questions," he said. "You know. About your family."

Well, that was nice while it lasted.

I thought he wanted me—not my family.

"You writing a magazine article?" I snapped. I didn't mean it to sound so cold, but it did.

Nate didn't seem to notice. He jammed his hands into his jeans pockets. "No. Things have been weird around here. I mean, some scary things happened to my friends and me. Like we were cursed or something. We almost drowned, you know. And then that girl in our class died. . . ."

His voice trailed off. I could see he was really messed up. But why did he think I had anything helpful to tell him?

I was shivering. I rubbed my arms. "Think I have to go inside," I said.

I turned—and saw a face pressed against the window, staring out. Ada. She was glaring at Nate and me.

Was she bad news or what?

"Look, Nate—," I started.

But he had turned away from me. He was staring up into the branches of a tall sycamore tree.

"Earth calling Nate," I said. "What's up there?"

"A bird," he said. He turned back to me, scratching his head. "I thought I saw a black-bird. I mean. Well . . . I guess it was just a shadow."

"You're into bird watching?" I said.

He didn't seem to hear me.

Ada still had her face pressed to the window glass. I decided to give her something to look at. I slid my arm around Nate's shoulders, pulled him close, and led him back into the house.

Jamie greeted me at the door. She squinted at me. "You and Nate?"

"Just talking," I said. "It's hard to hear in here."

"I need you," Jamie said, pulling me through the crowded living room. "I'm out of everything. Some guys went for pizza. Can you check the basement? See if you can find any more cans of Coke?"

"No problem," I said. I shivered. I couldn't shake off the cold from outside. "Just let me run up to my room and put on something warmer."

I bumped past Lewis, who was changing the CDs on the music system. Two couples were pressed together at the bottom of the stairs. They squirmed to the side so I could get upstairs.

I found a long-sleeved pullover in my dresser, tugged it on, and hurried back to help cousin Jamie. I stopped at the landing because someone was blocking the way.

Ada stood in front of me on the top step. She held a tray of glasses in front of her. The glasses tinkled as the tray shook in Ada's hands.

The bright ceiling light reflected off the glass, and I blinked. Whoa.

I suddenly felt dizzy, off-balance. The floor tilted, and the stairs appeared to rise up in front of me.

What a strange feeling. Why was the light reflecting so brightly? White light. Almost blinding.

I shut my eyes for a moment, trying to fight off the dizziness.

I opened them when I heard a shrill scream—and saw Ada falling . . . Ada tumbling . . . toppling headfirst down the staircase.

9

Screaming all the way, Ada thudded down the stairs.

The music and voices were so loud, but I could hear every *bump*, every time her head hit a wooden step.

And then the voices and singing and laughter stopped. As if someone had turned a switch. A few seconds after that, the music stopped too.

And now I felt as if I were swimming in silence, an ocean of silence. A bright white ocean of silence and light.

I grabbed the banister. I peered down through the billowing whiteness, forcing my eyes to focus.

And saw Ada. Crumpled up. Sprawled in a heap, surrounded by glittering lights. It took me a while to realize the lights were pieces of broken glass.

"Is she okay?" I screamed into the silence.

Kids were rushing to the stairway now, dropping down beside Ada. Brushing away the shards of shattered glass. Reaching for her. Eyes wide with worry and amazement.

Ada groaned. She slowly pushed herself up to a sitting position.

I saw bright red blood streaming down the front of her T-shirt and staining one sleeve. Bits of broken glass shimmered in her hair.

She groaned again and wiped her hands through her hair. Then, slowly, she raised her eyes to me.

I gasped when I saw the fierce anger on her face.

"You PUSHED me!" Ada screamed.

I heard gasps and low cries. All eyes were raised to me.

My legs felt wobbly, about to give way. I gripped the banister tightly to hold myself up. I felt my heart start to pound.

"N-no," I stammered, shaking my head. "I didn't touch you!"

Ada raised herself to her knees. She shook

a blood-smeared fist at me. "You DID, Dana!" she cried. "You shoved me!"

I couldn't help it. I burst into tears. "That's a LIE!" I cried. But my sobs muffled the words.

I gazed down from face to face. They all stared at me, accusing me. They *believed* her.

But I knew it wasn't true. I never touched her.

Why was she accusing me?

I couldn't stop sobbing. I turned and ran up the stairs. Back to my attic room, where I dropped into an armchair. I gripped the arms hard, gritted my teeth, and forced myself to stop crying.

From my room I could hear voices downstairs. But I couldn't make out the words. Were they all talking about me? Did they all believe Ada?

Why would I push her down the stairs? I had no reason to hurt her.

Did they think I pushed her because I want to steal Nate?

Nate is cute, but he isn't worth trying to *kill* someone!

Did they think I pushed her because I'm a Fear? And a member of the Fear family *has* to be evil? How stupid is *that*?

I heard the front door close. Heard voices in the driveway. Car doors slammed, and engines started up. The party was breaking up.

I was still hunched in the armchair, gritting my teeth, thinking angry thoughts, when Jamie came into my room. She hurried over and placed a hand on mine. "Dana, are you okay?"

"I . . . don't know," I said. I felt like crying again, but I forced it back.

Jamie squeezed my hand. "It was a good party," she said softly, "until Ada fell."

"I didn't push her!" I cried. I jerked Jamie's hand off mine. "Really. I never touched her."

Jamie nodded. "Of course you didn't."

I jumped to my feet. I balled my hands into tight fists. "So why did she accuse me like that?"

Jamie tossed back her dark hair. She suddenly looked so pale and tired. I could see that blue vein throbbing in her temple. "Ada will get over it," she said.

"Get over it?" I cried. "How? If she thinks I tried to kill her . . ."

"She was being emotional," Jamie replied. "Ada is very high-strung. When she thinks about it, she'll realize she made a mistake. She tripped, that's all."

"I . . . I felt weird up there," I confessed. "I was standing behind Ada at the top of the stairs. And the glasses on her tray suddenly started to shine in my eyes. I felt dizzy."

"Dizzy?"

"Yes. I thought I might black out. But . . . you've got to believe me. I didn't push her. I couldn't."

"Of course not," Jamie said in a soft, soothing voice. "Of course not."

So why was she staring at me so suspiciously?

10

The next couple of days I kept to myself. I was eager to find out what kind of greeting I'd get from everyone my first day at Shadyside High. But the school was closed for two days because of a water-main break.

Jamie hung out with Lewis and some of her other friends. And I heard her sneaking out after midnight to see her friends at the bar they all go to on Fear Street.

But I didn't feel like tagging along. Well, I guess I was a *little* tempted. I wanted to see Nate again. I kept thinking about him without even realizing it.

I wondered if he believed I pushed Ada down the stairs. I wondered if he'd be glad to see me, or if he'd try to avoid me.

But I didn't leave the house. I e-mailed

some friends from my old school. And I called my dad. Told him everything was just great. (As if he cared.) And I tried to read ahead in some of the school assignments.

The night before the high school was to open again, Jamie appeared in my room. "What's up?"

"Not much," I said. "Reading this Shakespeare play for English." I held up the book.

Jamie straightened some papers on my desk. "You nervous about tomorrow?"

"Kinda," I replied. "I'm sure your friends all think I'm some kind of monster because I'm a Fear and they think I pushed Ada down the stairs."

"No way," Jamie said, shaking her head. "No one is even talking about that anymore."

A lie. But a nice lie.

I couldn't get over the change in Jamie. How she was trying so hard to make me feel comfortable and everything.

Then she mentioned our cousin Cindy.

Cindy died in the hospital last August. She had been sick for a long time, but it was horrible and shocking. She was just a year older than Jamie and me.

"I saw Cindy a week before she died," Jamie said, settling on the edge of my bed. "Did you see her?"

"No. I was too far away," I replied, putting down my book. "But I talked to her on the phone. She . . . she said she was getting stronger. I knew she was just being brave."

I sighed. "She died three days later. When I heard, I cried and cried. She was such a cool person."

Jamie's eyes narrowed. She had a cold expression on her face, an expression I'd never seen before. "Life can really suck," she whispered.

We stared at each other for a long moment. My ears started to ring. I waited for Jamie to break the silence. When she didn't, I said, "You know, Cindy was a Fear too."

A strange smile spread over Jamie's lips. "I know." She picked at the strings around the hole on the knee of her jeans. "Dana, did Cindy say anything to you about sending a signal?"

I narrowed my eyes at her. "A signal? No."

Jamie tugged at the knee of her jeans. "Cindy promised me she'd send a signal," she said, her voice just above a whisper.

It took me a while to understand. "You mean a signal from the grave?"

Jamie nodded. "She promised. She said she'd send me a sign from the other side. I've been watching for it ever since . . . ever since she died."

I leaned forward in my chair. "And?"

"Nothing yet. But I keep watching. And I keep trying to reach her." Jamie crossed her arms in front of her. "Do you believe in ghosts?"

I laughed. "Because I'm a Fear?"

Jamie didn't smile. "No. Do you believe in spirits?"

"I . . . don't think so," I said. "I mean, I never think about stuff like that."

"I do," Jamie said. "I believe in spirits. I *want* to believe in them. I want to contact Cindy's spirit. I want her promise to come true."

I stared at Jamie. This wasn't like her at all. When I knew her, she was a spoiled rich kid, and kind of a bubblehead. She thought mostly about her hair and boys and buying new clothes. I never knew she was into the supernatural.

"Why?" I asked.

"Because I miss her so much," Jamie said. She jumped to her feet and pulled me up. "Come downstairs."

I followed her down the stairs. I saw flickering lights from her room. Stepping into the doorway, I saw that the room was dark—except for the dancing flames of five candles set up on the floor in a circle. Five black candles.

I hesitated. "Jamie—?"

She shoved me into the room and carefully closed the door behind us. The room smelled spicy, as if she'd been burning incense. The candle flames sent flickering light to the walls, and I saw a giant *Buffy* poster over Jamie's bed.

Jamie motioned for me to sit down in front of the candles. She dropped beside me and sat cross-legged. The orange light flickered and danced over her pale face, her dark eyes glowing with excitement.

"I've been teaching myself magic," she said, staring straight ahead into the firelight.

"You mean to contact Cindy?"

She nodded. She slid an old book out from under her bed. The cover was cracked and torn. She opened it carefully, flipping through the brittle pages.

"I found this old spellbook," she whispered. "I've been trying different spells. I know I can contact her."

I felt a chill tighten the back of my neck. This wasn't like the Jamie I remembered. Cindy's death must have hit her really hard.

"Do your parents know about this?" I asked, staring into the darting orange light.

"Of course not," Jamie whispered. "They never come upstairs."

She ran her finger down a long column of type in the old book. "Dana, we can do it," she said. "Let's try and contact Cindy together."

"Okay," I replied, feeling another chill.

Did I have a choice? She was kinda freaking me out. But *no way* I could jump up and leave.

We held hands. We leaned toward the circle of black candles.

Jamie held the book in her lap. She whispered some words in a language I didn't recognize. Then she began to chant in a loud whisper: "Cindy, where are you? Cindy, where are you . . . ?"

I took a deep breath and joined in. "Cindy, where are you? Cindy, where are you? Cindy, where are you?"

Holding hands, the firelight washing over us, we chanted the phrase over and over. "Cindy, where are you . . . ?"

And then my heart skipped a beat when I heard a soft reply from close by: *"I'm here . . . I'm HERE!"*

11

I raised my eyes to Jamie. She stared back at me, eyes wide, her mouth hanging open. She had heard it too.

I raised myself to my knees. In my excitement, I almost knocked over one of the candles.

"Cindy? Is that you?" Jamie whispered.

And again we heard the soft whisper of a voice, so close . . . so close to us: *"I'm here . . . I'm here."*

I froze, blinking into the flickering flames.

Jamie jumped to her feet. Her eyes narrowed. "Wait a minute," she murmured.

She tiptoed to her closet, pulled open the door—and Danny came tumbling out. "You RAT!" Jamie screamed.

It took me a few seconds to realize that Danny had been the whisperer.

Jamie grabbed the little guy, and he started to giggle. Jamie wrestled him to the floor and tickled his stomach with both hands. He wriggled on his back, giggling and slapping at Jamie.

"You rat! You rat!" Jamie cried, laughing with her brother.

"You scared me to *death*!" I confessed.

Danny rolled out of his sister's grasp. He jumped to his feet and sprinted to the doorway.

"How long were you in there?" Jamie demanded.

He didn't answer. He giggled some more, totally pleased with his little joke. Then he disappeared into the hall. We heard him clumping down the stairs, shouting, "Hey, Mom! Mom! I played a joke on Jamie and Dana!"

Jamie dropped back onto her knees on the carpet and began to blow out the candles. "Guess we won't reach Cindy tonight," she said.

"Think Danny knew what we were doing?" I asked.

She shrugged. "Who knows *what* Danny knows? He's such a funny kid."

"Yeah, funny," I said. My heart was still pounding.

• • •

My first day at Shadyside High was as hard as I'd expected. I mean, how impossible is it to start a new school senior year?

Jamie gave me a short tour of the building before classes started. But of course I forgot everything she told me as soon as she hurried off to homeroom.

I kept staring at faces, looking for kids I knew. I actually remembered some kids from elementary school, but they didn't seem to remember me.

I saw Nate in the hall between third and fourth period. I hurried over to him, but he was rushing somewhere with his friend Shark. We barely said hi.

After school, I found Ada and Whitney in front of their lockers. They were both talking at once. But when they saw me coming, they stopped and both put these fake smiles on their faces.

Whitney wore a short, pleated skirt and layers of T-shirts. Ada had a maroon and gray Shadyside High sweatshirt pulled down over very tight, boot-cut jeans.

"How's it going, Dana?" Whitney asked, eyeing me up and down.

I sighed. "I was late to two classes. I couldn't find the rooms. My school was all on one level, not three floors."

Ada snickered. "Jamie should've drawn you a map."

"I guess," I said. "I'm sure I'll figure it all out in a few days."

Ada shifted her backpack on her shoulders. She was staring at me coldly.

I wanted to apologize for the other night at Jamie's party. I wanted to find out if she still thought I had pushed her down the stairs. I didn't want one of Jamie's friends as an enemy.

But how could I bring it up?

Besides, I was late for an after-school try-out.

"Where is the music room?" I asked them. "I'm totally turned around. I'm supposed to be there now. I'm trying out for chorus."

Ada's mouth dropped open. "Whitney and I are in the chorus," she said. "It's all filled up."

She said it so coldly, as if I had no business even asking her about it.

"My chorus teacher from back home sent a note to Ms. Watson," I explained. "She told her about the singing awards I've won."

"So Ms. Watson said you could try out?" Ada asked.

I nodded. "Yes. She's waiting for me in the music room." I held up both hands with my fingers crossed. "I really need to be in chorus," I told them. "Because I'm trying out for the Collingsworth Music Scholarship."

They both gasped. They exchanged glances. "Ada and I are both trying for the Collingsworth Prize," Whitney said. They glared at me. They didn't even try to hide their feelings.

"I'm sorry," I said. "I guess we'll be competing against one another."

"Guess we will," Ada muttered.

"If I don't win it, I won't be able to go to college," I said. I don't know why I told them that. It was very personal. I guess I was trying to make them my friends.

The Collingsworth Music Scholarship is a statewide scholarship. It includes singing and academics. You have to have a really good grade point average to apply.

I'm a good student, and I know how to get good grades. But sometimes I clutch at test time. I didn't do that well on my SATs.

My singing is the one thing I'm confident

about. I hoped I was good enough to win the scholarship. Otherwise, I'd have to get a job after high school.

Ada and Whitney were still frowning at me. "Only two students can be sent from each high school," Ada said. "We can only send two kids to compete at the state level."

"I know," I said. I didn't know what else to say. Of course it meant that all three of us couldn't win.

I glanced at my watch. "I'm really late," I said. "Can you direct me to the music room?"

They kept staring at me, letting me know they didn't like me. Ada rubbed her shoulder. "It still hurts from the other night," she said. "Something is pulled. I have to have X-rays."

"I'm sorry," I told her. Then I added, "I didn't push you. I would never do anything like that."

She didn't reply to that. Instead, she pointed down the hall. "Keep going that way to the end. You'll find it."

"Thanks," I said. I turned and hurried off.

"Good luck," Whitney called, totally sarcastic.

"Yeah, good luck," Ada shouted. "Break a leg!"

12

The school was emptying. Kids were going home. I jogged down the long hall, dodging a group of cheerleaders carrying silver batons.

I thought about Ada and Whitney. What a shame we'd be competing for the scholarship prize. I realized I'd never win them over as friends.

I could tell they really believed I pushed Ada down those stairs. Is that what *everyone* in school believes?

How unlucky to start out life at Shadyside High with everyone suspecting me. And all because of a misunderstanding.

I tried to force those thoughts from my mind. I had to keep cool and concentrate on impressing Ms. Watson. Making friends was not as important as winning the money to go to college.

Ms. Watson was a tall woman, young and very pretty, with shiny, blue eyes, high cheekbones like a model, and light blond hair pulled back in a French braid. She wore a pale blue turtleneck over tight, charcoal slacks that showed off her long legs.

As I entered, she looked up from her desk, where she was sorting through a stack of sheet music. She had a killer smile. "Are you Dana?"

I nodded. "Yes. Sorry, I'm late. I couldn't find this room."

She crossed the room and shook hands with me. She was at least a head taller than me! I barely came up to her shoulders. "Your first day?" she asked.

"It seems like *ten* days," I replied. "I spent most of the day totally lost."

"Well, come over here." She led the way to her desk. She had a music stand set up beside it. "You certainly come highly recommended. What's-his-name—Mr. Margolis? He couldn't stop praising you in his letter."

"He's really nice," I said. Hearing my old music teacher's name gave me a pang of homesickness.

Ms. Watson picked up the letter from her

desk. "This is an impressive list of singing awards, Dana. Did you bring music with you?"

"No. I have some things memorized," I said. My throat tightened. I suddenly felt cold, nervous. The feeling I always have before singing.

"I have a song from *The Vagabond King*," I told her. "You know. The operetta. And I have a Bach piece we used to use as a warm-up."

"Excellent," Ms. Watson said, flashing me that smile again. I want the name of her teeth-whitener, I thought. She motioned me to the music stand and took a seat behind her desk. "Anytime you're ready, Dana."

I cleared my throat. As I turned to the front of the room, I saw something move in the doorway. The classroom door was open a little more than a crack. I could see a person standing there. And I recognized her by her red hair.

Ada.

Hiding there. Spying on me from the hall.

I took a deep breath. Anger pushed away all my nervousness.

Okay, Ada, I thought. If you want to see a show, I'll give you a show.

I don't think I ever sang better. My voice was clear and steady. I don't think I wavered on a single note. And all the while I could see Ada hunched at the door, eavesdropping on my performance.

When I finished the second piece, Ms. Watson applauded. "Dana, I'm impressed," she said, standing up and shaking my hand again. "Mr. Margolis didn't exaggerate. You really have a gift."

"Thank you," I said. "I've been singing since I was a little girl. My mother heard me singing along with a CD when I was three or something. She couldn't believe I was hitting all the notes. So she started me with lessons."

"You should congratulate your mother," Ms. Watson said. "That was very wise of her."

"I can't," I blurted out. "She died a few months ago."

Ms. Watson's cheeks turned bright pink. "Oh, I'm sorry." She bit her bottom lip. Her bright blue eyes locked on mine.

"Anyway," she said, "we need you desperately in our chorus. I know the others will be so happy to have you join us."

I glanced at the doorway. Ada hadn't

moved. I wondered what she was thinking. Probably making hex signs.

"Thank you," I said. "You'll have to show me what you've been singing. It'll probably take me a while to catch up."

Ms. Watson returned to her desk and sifted through a file of papers. "Dana, have you applied for the Collingsworth Prize? I think I have an application for it here."

"Thank you. I've already filled it out," I told her.

I thought I heard Ada groan from behind the doorway.

"Well, this school is naming two finalists," Ms. Watson said. "I think you have a real chance."

It was my turn to blush. She was being so awesomely nice.

"I'll try," I said.

She handed me a schedule of chorus rehearsals. I thanked her again and strode out of the room. I swung the door open wide.

Ada must have been frozen there or something. She hadn't moved.

Behind me, Ms. Watson let out a startled cry. "Ada? Are you still in school?"

Ada blinked several times, as if coming out of a daze. "Uh . . . yeah. I had to stay after," she said.

"Do you have a minute? I want to talk to you," Ms. Watson said, motioning for Ada to come in. "Have you met Dana?"

Ada didn't look at me. "Yeah. We've met."

"I've got to run," I said. I pushed past Ada and hurried out the door. I pulled the door shut after me—but only partway.

It was *my* turn to eavesdrop!

I gripped the doorknob and stepped back from the opening. I kept glancing up and down the hall, making sure no one was approaching. But it was nearly four o'clock. The hall was empty.

I leaned into the doorway and listened.

"I don't understand," Ada was saying. She didn't sound happy.

Ms. Watson replied in a low, steady voice. "I'm saying you have to bring your singing up to the next level, Ada. Or I'm afraid you won't make the finals."

"But . . ." Ada hesitated. "Ms. Watson, you practically *guaranteed* that I'd go to the state finals."

"Well, I didn't really guarantee it," the teacher replied. "And, I have to be honest with you, Ada. The competition has just gotten a lot tougher."

Silence for a long moment. Then Ada said, "You mean Dana?"

"Yes," Ms. Watson replied. "Dana has had a lot of training. I can't lie: I was impressed by her. She's a very strong singer."

"But that isn't *fair*!" Ada was whining now. "She's too late, isn't she? She can't just transfer here and—"

"Dana is definitely eligible," the teacher replied. "Take it easy, Ada. You're getting yourself all worked up over nothing. You can still qualify. You just have to work hard. Practice a lot more. Concentrate your efforts."

Again, Ada was silent. Then she muttered something too low for me to hear.

She came storming out, shoving the door in front of her. I staggered back. Her face was bright red, and her mouth was set in an angry scowl.

I don't know if she saw me or not. She spun the other way and strode down the hall, her shoes thudding loudly on the concrete floor.

Now I *definitely* have made an enemy, I told myself.

I suddenly pictured Jamie. Jamie and Ada were such good friends. I knew Jamie wouldn't want Ada and me to be at each other's throats.

I decided to go after Ada and talk to her. Tell her I really wanted us to be friends. See if I could convince her to start all over.

I trotted down the long, empty hall. My footsteps echoed against the tile walls and banks of metal lockers.

I turned the corner and gazed down another long hall. No sign of Ada.

How did she disappear so fast? I wondered.

And then I let out a scream as someone grabbed me hard from behind.

13

I spun around. "Nate! What are you doing here?"

He grinned at me. He has a cute, lopsided grin. "Sorry. Didn't mean to scare you."

"Yes, you did," I teased. "You like to make girls scream, don't you?"

His grin grew wider. "Maybe."

"So why are you still here?"

He shrugged. "Shark and I had detention. Don't ask."

I narrowed my eyes at him. "Nate, I thought you were a *good* boy."

He grinned again. "I can be *very* good."

I could see he liked me teasing him like that, coming on to him. Did I have a crush on him already? My mind was spinning.

Stay away from him, Dana. Ada already hates you. Don't make it worse.

"So? What's up?" I asked. I started walking to my locker.

He hurried after me. "These guys . . . uh . . . they're having a skating party Saturday night. On Fear Lake."

Fear Lake. I hadn't thought about that lake on the other side of the woods since I was a kid. My family used to have picnics on the shore. And my dad would drag a canoe there and we'd paddle around for hours.

The memories rushed back to me. Fun times. Before we moved away. Before it all turned bad. . . .

"Is the lake frozen already?" I asked.

Nate nodded. "Yeah. It's been so cold this fall."

"I'm not a great ice-skater," I said. "Weak ankles."

He raised his eyes to mine. "You're probably better than me. The last time Shark and I went skating, I fell on top of a six-year-old girl. It was totally embarrassing."

I laughed. I stopped at my locker. I stared at the lock, trying to remember the combination.

"So . . . you want to go?" Nate asked. "You know. With me?"

I turned back to him. "What about Ada?"

His smile faded. "I *told* you. She doesn't own me." He pulled down the neck of his T-shirt. "See? No leash."

I pictured Ada and Whitney staring at me so coldly. "Well . . ."

"I like you," Nate blurted out. "You're interesting."

"Thanks for the compliment," I said. "Okay. I'll go."

That brought the smile back to his face. But I immediately regretted it.

What did he mean, I was *interesting*?

Was Nate interested in *me*? Or was he interested because he thought I could tell him stories about the Fear family?

I had to talk to Jamie.

I needed advice on what to do about Ada. And I needed advice about Nate.

My first day at Shadyside High, and already I felt in the middle of something. Maybe Nate was someone I could really be into. Maybe he was someone I could trust, someone to rely on.

Or was he someone I should stay away from?

Jamie would tell me.

I hurried home. The sun had already lowered behind the trees. I hate winter. I hate when it gets dark so early.

I looked for Jamie in her room. I saw her backpack and her bag tossed on the floor by her bed, so I knew she was home. But no sign of her.

Jamie's mom—my aunt Audra—was in the den. She looks like an older version of Jamie, with wavy, black hair and creamy, white skin. She had classical music on the stereo. She was lying on the couch, doing a crossword puzzle.

"Jamie is in her studio," she told me. "You know. In the garage. Ever since the accident, that's where she spends her time. Doing pottery she never lets me see."

Did I detect a little bitterness there?

I thanked her and headed to the back of the house.

"Dana, how was your first day?" Aunt Audra called after me.

"Great!" I shouted back. No sense getting into it.

I closed the kitchen door behind me and stepped onto the driveway. A gusting wind had come up, shaking the bare trees in the backyard. A shutter rattled at the side of the house.

I was still wearing my down jacket from school. I pulled up the collar as I trotted to the garage.

The single, pull-down door was shut. The door had no window, but I could see yellow light pouring out at the side of the garage.

"Hey, Jamie!" I shouted, cupping my hands around my mouth. "It's me!" I listened hard. No reply. "Hey—Jamie?"

I bent down, grabbed the garage door handle, and started to hoist up the heavy door.

I had it raised a foot or so from the driveway when I heard the loud shriek from inside:

"Stay OUT! I mean it! STAY OUT!"

14

"Jamie, it's me," I called. "Are you okay?"

I heard running footsteps. The garage door rolled up a few feet. Jamie slid outside and pushed the door down behind her.

Her face was red, and she was breathing hard.

I jumped back. "Sorry. Why did you scream like that? You . . . you scared me."

She had a towel in one hand, covered with brown and red stains. She used it to wipe a spot of clay off one cheek.

"I'm sorry too," she said. "I didn't mean to scream. It's just . . . well . . . I don't allow anyone in my sculpture studio."

I narrowed my eyes at her. "Excuse me?"

"It's kinda my own private space," she said, balling up the towel between her hands. "It's my therapy. After the accident . . . after I fell into that excavation hole last year, I was home for months. I needed a lot of rehab time. I turned this studio into my own private world."

I still didn't understand why I couldn't come in and see what she was doing. But no point in arguing with her. She had a rough year, after all. She's entitled to her own space.

She studied me for a moment. "Dana, how was your first day at our lovely school?"

"Just *lovely*," I said. I grabbed the sleeve of her sweatshirt. "Can I talk to you for a minute or two?"

She nodded. "Sure. Give me a sec to clean up. I'll meet you in the kitchen."

When she joined me at the kitchen table a few minutes later, she still had a spot of red clay on one cheek. She dropped down across from me and rolled up her sweatshirt sleeves.

"You're sweating," I said.

"It's hot in there," she said, mopping her forehead with the back of her hand. "It's the kiln. Dad went a little crazy. He got me the biggest kiln they make, I think. It's like a blast furnace."

She jumped up, jogged to the fridge, and came back with a bottle of water. After downing half the bottle, she turned to me. "So? What's up? Your first day at Shadyside High. Details, please."

I told her about being lost and a little overwhelmed by the size of the place. And I told her about a couple of cute guys I met in the library.

She stuck her finger down her throat and made gagging sounds. "I know those guys. They're not cute once you get to know them."

I laughed. "Yeah, I know they're not the clean-cut, straight-arrow type like Lewis. But I like punky guys."

She shrugged. "Whatever." She brushed her wavy, dark hair off one eye. "So what did you want to talk to me about?"

"Well, I found out something kinda bad after school," I began. I told her about running into Ada and Whitney on my way to my audition with Ms. Watson. And I told her how I'd applied for the Collingsworth Prize.

"Uh-oh," Jamie muttered, squeezing the plastic water bottle in her hand. "Ada and Whitney applied too."

"You got it," I said.

Jamie took another long slug of water, keeping her eyes on me. "Ada has to be furious," she said. "She thinks she has that scholarship prize aced."

"I know," I said. "That's strike two for me with your friend Ada."

Jamie frowned. "Or maybe strike three," she said. "Ada looks like a little mouse, but she has an awesome temper. Red hair, you know."

"I got off to a *horrible* start with Ada," I said. "I know she's your good friend. I don't want her to hate me. But I *have* to win that prize, Jamie."

Her mouth dropped open. I guess I was a little intense.

"Don't you understand? If I don't win that prize," I said, "I'll have to go to work. I won't be able to go to college."

Jamie nodded. "Yeah, I know, Dana."

"I feel bad for Ada," I said. "But I'll do *anything* to win."

Jamie stared hard at me. "Anything?"

"Well . . . ," I replied. "Yeah. Anything."

15

I guess I had a few beers. I was feeling pretty good. I mean, there I was at a table full of guys. It was about one A.M. on Wednesday night, and none of the other girls had come into Nights yet.

I was kicking back, having a nice time, flirting with all of them. Nate had an arm draped over my shoulder. Shark kept pulling out his cell, calling that girl Nikki, asking why she wasn't coming tonight. Lewis and Galen kept tossing popcorn in the air, trying to see who could catch the most in their mouths.

"Who started this idea of sneaking out late at night?" I asked.

"Is it night?" Shark joked. "No wonder it's so dark!" He'd had more beers than I had.

"Jamie and I started it," Lewis said. He was

the only one drinking Diet Cokes. "We called ourselves the Night People."

"Clever name," Galen said. "Did you think of that all by yourself?"

Lewis ignored him. "Jamie and I started sneaking out before this bar was built. We used to meet inside the old Fear Mansion, right on this spot."

Galen rolled his eyes. "Tell us something we *don't* know." He slid out of the booth and walked up to the front to get another beer from Ryland O'Connor.

"Pretty soon these copycats started sneaking out too," Lewis told me. "Jamie and I can't get any privacy."

Shark jabbed Lewis in the ribs. "And why do you need privacy?" he teased.

We all laughed.

"Well, this is so cool," I gushed. "We have secret night lives no one knows about."

Shark leaned into me. "Tell us some secrets, Dana."

"No way," I said, pushing him away.

"Come on. Give us a break. Tell us some dirty secrets." He took a long pull from his beer bottle.

"Shark, you always act like this after half a beer?" I said.

Everyone laughed again, even Ryland from behind the bar.

Galen brought refills for everyone. Nate lowered his hand from my shoulder to take his beer. "So you didn't do this back home?" he asked.

I shook my head. "My parents would have *killed* me. I can't believe your parents haven't found out."

"My parents are divorced," Nate said. "That means I have only *one* parent to fool. And she works all day, so it would take a bomb blast to wake her up."

"My parents drink themselves to sleep," Shark said. "It's not much of a challenge to sneak out."

"Lucky," Galen said.

Lewis kept gazing at the front door. Maybe he was expecting Jamie to show.

Nate squeezed my hand. "So what did you do for laughs back home?"

I shoved his hand away. "None of your business. You're too young."

The other guys hee-hawed at that one.

The five of us kidded around for a while. I could tell Nate was really into me. Just by the way he kept touching me and giving me looks.

I was attracted to him too. But one thing bummed me out—the way he kept getting serious, asking me questions about my life back home and what it was like being a Fear.

What was his *problem*, anyway?

Finally, he told me about some weird things that had happened to him in October. The stories were totally bizarre. He said one night at the bar, cockroaches started pouring out of his mouth. And then one day in school, both of his ears started spurting blood for no reason at all.

Yikes.

He said everyone believed Candy Shutt was using Angelica Fear's amulet to cast spells on him. But it turned out not to be true.

Was someone else doing these things to Nate?

Was there someone out there who knew how to put curses on people? Someone who really wanted to hurt Nate and his friends?

The whole idea sounded crazy to me.

"You're a Fear, right?" Nate said, squeezing my arm. "Do you know spells and sorcery and stuff? Do you know how to do things to people you hate?"

I just stared at him. My head was kinda buzzing from the beers I'd drunk. And my eyes weren't totally focusing.

But I could think straight enough to know that I didn't like his questions.

I shoved my beer bottle in front of him. "Drink some more," I snapped. "Maybe you'll make more sense."

"No. Really—," he started.

"Nate, I don't know what you're talking about," I told him. "How would I know anything about that? Just because I'm a Fear doesn't mean I'm interested in—"

"Sorry. Sorry," he said. He leaned over and kissed me on the cheek. "Sorry. Really. Sorry. Umm, did I say I was sorry?"

Shark laughed. "Kiss her again, Nate."

I glanced up—and saw Ada staring at us from the middle of the room.

Did she see Nate kiss me?

Yes. It was easy to tell from the angry scowl on her face.

"Hey, Ada—," Nate started. "Scoot over, Shark. Make room—"

But before anyone could move, Ada grabbed Nate by the arm and pulled him from the booth. He had a goofy, confused look on his face. He half-stumbled, half-shuffled after her. I saw her pin him to the wall next to the bathrooms.

"Ada, want a beer?" Shark shouted. He grinned at me. The whole thing was a joke to him.

But I had this heavy feeling in the pit of my stomach. And my head started to buzz even louder.

The three guys at my table all started talking at once. But they didn't drown out Ada.

I could hear her getting into Nate's face. I couldn't hear her words because she was speaking in a loud whisper. But you didn't have to be a genius to figure out what she was saying.

And then I heard these words from Nate: "I'm just trying to be nice to her. It's tough being the new kid."

Ow. That hurt.

And then I heard Ada's furious reply: "Don't be *too* nice to her. Hear me?"

Whoa.

After that, it got ugly. The two of them started shouting at each other. Ada no longer cared if I heard or not.

I jumped to my feet when I heard her scream, "She's trying to take my boyfriend *and* my scholarship!"

I saw the smile fade from Shark's face. He lurched over to break it up.

But I didn't care. I'd heard enough. No way I was going to sit there and pretend it wasn't all about me.

I turned and ran. Ran down the long bar, pushed open the front door, and darted out into the cold, clear night.

Breathing hard. My heart pounding. I watched my breath puff up in front of me. And I cried out loud to the empty street, "What am I going to do about Ada?"

16

Saturday night a fog settled over Fear Lake, giving it an eerie, dreamlike feel. Pale rays of moonlight poked through the billowing fog, making dappled spots over the ice.

It was my turn to keep an eye on Jamie's little brother Danny for a few hours. So the skating party was underway by the time I arrived.

Some kids had set up tents at the edge of the frozen lake. They were serving hot chocolate from big, silver urns, and I saw cans of soda and beer stacked in another tent. A small bonfire sent up orange and yellow flames into the foggy sky.

A guy I recognized from school stood behind two turntables and a pair of loudspeakers. He must have had a portable generator. His music blasted out over the voices of kids skating, clustered in couples and groups, and huddled near the tents.

It hadn't snowed yet this fall, but the lake appeared frozen solid, and the ground along the shore was crunchy and hard. Chunks of frost crinkled under my boots.

I wore two sweaters under my parka, a long, striped scarf around my neck, and a wool ski cap pulled down over my ears, but I still shivered from the frigid, damp air.

"Hey, Dana—yo!"

I turned and saw Jamie standing with Lewis at the edge of the ice. I hurried over to them.

I had Jamie's skates slung over my shoulder. Jamie couldn't use them because her hip and leg weren't recovered enough to skate.

"Nate was looking for you," Lewis said. He pointed with his soda can to a group of kids huddled under a tree, singing along at the top of their voices with the DJ's cranked-up music.

I recognized Nate. He motioned for me to join him.

Jamie squinted at me. "You're here with Nate?"

I just waved my hand. I didn't answer. I

turned and half-ran, half-slid over to Nate and his friends. As I drew closer, I recognized Shark and Nikki, and Aaron and Galen. They all waved and called out to me.

I slid right into Nate. Laughing, he caught me around the waist. He held on to me for a little while, which I didn't mind at all.

"Are we having fun yet?" Shark asked.

The fog swirled around us. Circles of yellow moonlight slid over the frozen lake. It was hard to see where the shore ended and the lake began.

"Dana, want a beer?" Nate reached for a six-pack beside him on the ground.

"No thanks," I said. I swung Jamie's skates off my shoulder. "You just going to stand here drinking beer? I thought we were going to skate."

"Some of us came for the beer," Shark said.

Nikki gave him a hard shove. "You promised we'd skate. You told me you're a killer skater. You said you made the state hockey finals last year."

Aaron and Galen tossed back their heads and laughed.

"I'm totally shocked," Nate said. "Shark *never* lied before!"

More laughter.

"Maybe I exaggerated about my skating a little," Shark confessed.

Nikki glared at him. "Tell the truth. Have you ever been on ice skates?"

Shark hesitated. He grinned at Nikki. "Do they go on your feet, or what?"

Nikki gave him another shove.

"Hey, I can still skate better than Nate," Shark told her.

"No way," Nate said. "Want to make a bet on it?"

"Can't we just skate for fun and party tonight without any bets?" I asked, leaning against Nate.

"What do you want to bet?" Shark asked Nate, ignoring me. "How about the rest of that beer?"

He grabbed the can from Nate's hand, tilted it to his mouth, and drained it. "See? I won the bet already!"

Nikki shook her head at Shark. "How not funny are you?"

He kissed her. "You love it," he said.

"Well, I'm putting on my skates," I told Nate. "Are you coming with me?"

He nodded.

I pulled him to a bench at the edge of the lake. We strapped on our skates, watching kids already on the ice. They appeared to float through the swirls of fog.

Couples skated together in graceful circles. One guy took a running jump, dove forward, and went sliding headfirst at full speed over the ice into a group of girls.

They scattered, squealing and laughing.

"That's Dan Nickerson," Nate told me. "He does that every year."

"Cute," I said.

Nate pulled me to my feet, and we skated out onto the lake. We made wide circles at first, skating slowly. I hadn't been on ice skates in years, but it quickly came back to me.

Nate was a pretty good skater. But he kept grabbing my hand to steady his balance. We were far out on the lake. At least, it seemed far out. Squinting through the fog, I could barely see the tents and the kids on the shore.

Nate grabbed my gloved hand and held on. We slowed to a stop. He pulled me close and kissed me. I kissed him back. I let him know I was enjoying it.

How long did we kiss?

I don't know. I pulled away from him when I heard someone shouting my name. Breathless, I turned and saw Jamie running across the ice toward us.

She was limping and sliding, waving her arms to keep her balance. "Dana? Is that you?" she called.

I broke away from Nate and took a few sliding steps toward her. "Jamie, what's wrong?"

"Ada," she gasped, struggling to catch her breath. She bent over, pressing her hands on her knees.

"What about Ada?" Nate asked.

"She's here," Jamie said, pointing to the shore. "She's looking for you, Dana. She found out you're here with Nate."

I squinted at her. "Excuse me?"

"I mean, she's out of control. So mad!" Jamie said. "I just wanted to warn you."

"Oh, wow," I muttered.

Jamie limped away, shaking her head.

I saw a blur of movement to her left. Through the curtain of fog, I recognized Ada, bent low, skating fast.

Nate shook his head angrily. "Forget it," he said. "I don't need this."

"But, wait—," I protested. "Don't leave me here." My heart started to pound in my chest.

He skated off, head down, taking long strides.

"That's not fair!" I shouted.

Ada came roaring toward me. She wore layers of sweaters over tight jeans. Her long scarf flew behind her like a flag.

"Ada—stop!" I cried.

"You can't have him!" she shouted. "You can't come here and ruin my life!"

Sobbing, she bumped me hard. I toppled backward. But she grabbed me and held me up.

"Ada—please!"

She grabbed my shoulders and started to shake me.

"Let go! Let go!" I screamed, struggling to squirm away.

But she lowered her gloved hands and curled them around my throat. "You can't! You can't!" she uttered.

"Ada—*stop*!" I pleaded as her fingers tightened. I suddenly felt dizzy. I couldn't breathe.

"Stop! You're *choking* me!"

17

I opened my eyes. I blinked a few times, trying to focus.

I felt so dizzy. My ears rang.

Had I blacked out or something?

I took a deep breath and gazed around. I was sitting on the ice, with my legs spread. My throat ached. My heart pounded hard.

I shut my eyes again. Why did I feel so wiped? So weak, I couldn't raise my arms?

When I opened my eyes again, I could see kids skating toward me, their faces hidden in the thickening fog. I heard shouts, but I couldn't understand the words.

Confused, I tried to pull myself up. But I sank back onto the ice, my head spinning.

What *happened* to me?

Jamie's voice broke through the ringing in

my ears. I felt her gloved hand on my shoulder.
I turned and gazed up into her worried face.

"Dana, we heard screams. Where's Ada?"

Huh? Ada?

Jamie turned away from me. Her mouth
dropped open, and she squeezed my shoulder
so hard, I gasped.

I turned to see what she was staring at. And
uttered a sharp cry.

Ada?

Yes. Stretched out on her back on the ice.

Ada . . . Ada in a dark pool of blood.

Ada with an ice skate . . . the blade . . . the
blade . . . driven into her head. Standing straight
up. Poking out from between her open, glassy
eyes.

Without realizing it, I jumped to my feet.

I saw Jamie's accusing stare.

I raised my gloved hands to the sides of my
face and I started to scream: "I didn't do it! I
didn't do it! I didn't do it . . . !"

PART THREE

PART THREE

18

I've had some hard times lately, with my mom dying and my dad deciding he didn't want me to live with him. And some other painful stuff.

But the next three days were a total nightmare, the worst days of my life.

The Shadyside police showed up about ten minutes after we saw Ada's body. You can imagine the screams of horror and crying and wailing that went on when the other kids all came skating out to take a look at her. And the cold, accusing stares I got.

Every kid there thought I was a murderer.

Including Nate and Jamie, I'm sure.

At least, Jamie stood by me. I don't remember seeing Nate. He simply disappeared.

Anyway, the police took me to their precinct

station in the Old Village. They called Jamie's parents. Her dad is a lawyer, thank goodness.

We all sat around a beat–up, metal table in a tiny, gray room. Everyone grim and yellow–faced under harsh fluorescent ceiling lights.

Jamie's mother kept her eyes down. She wouldn't look at me. Mr. Richards squeezed my hand and whispered that I didn't have to answer any questions I didn't want to.

"I-I'll answer what I can," I stammered.

Two police officers—a man and a woman—questioned me for hours. I told them everything I could.

The last thing I remembered was Ada leaping on me and choking me. I told them I remembered the feeling of her wool gloves, scratchy on my neck. How she tightened her fingers around my throat. How she cut off my windpipe.

I couldn't breathe.

I pleaded with her to let go.

That's all. Nothing more to tell.

The next thing I knew, I was sitting up on the ice, feeling dazed. My head felt as if it weighed a hundred pounds, and my eyes wouldn't focus.

I must have blacked out because Ada cut off my air. She tried to choke me to death. I tried to get away. I tried to free myself.

But I didn't fight back. And I didn't kill her.

We went over and over the whole thing. I think the two officers wanted to trick me into changing my story. Or they thought maybe I'd break down and confess.

They checked my neck. And yes, there were red bruises at my throat, just as I'd said.

I had tears streaming down my cheeks. I kept drinking cup after cup of water. My hands shook. I clasped them tightly in my lap and stared across the table at the two cops.

I looked straight into their eyes. I wanted to convince them I was telling the truth.

And finally, I raised my trembling hands. "Look at my hands," I said. "Look at my arms. I don't work out or anything. Look how skinny I am. I'm not strong enough to shove a skate blade through someone's skull. No way."

I held my arms up, and they stared at them. Studied them. I think maybe it helped convince them.

"I was being choked to death," I told them.

"I couldn't breathe. I couldn't fight her off. How could I unlace her skate and drive it through her head?"

"I think we're going to end this now," Jamie's dad said. "Are you going to charge Dana?"

The two officers whispered to each other. Then they left the room.

I turned to Jamie's mom. Mrs. Richards had a handkerchief pressed to her face. I couldn't see her expression.

Mr. Richards patted my hand. "I think they believe you," he murmured. "Did you see anyone else around? Do you know of someone else who had a grudge against Ada or might want to see her dead?"

I stared at him. I'd already answered those questions for the police officers. "No. I don't remember anyone," I said again.

He nodded. "Dana, have you had blackouts before?" he asked.

"No one ever tried to strangle me before," I answered.

But I suddenly remembered that strange, woozy feeling I'd had at the top of the stairs at Jamie's party. I felt so weird that night, as if I was blacking out. And the next thing I knew, I was staring down the stairs at Ada, sprawled on the landing on top of all that broken glass.

I didn't mention it to Jamie's dad. But for the first time all night, the question popped quietly into my mind: *Did* I kill Ada?

Did I go into some kind of weird blackout and murder her without even knowing it?

No.

No way.

No. No. No.

The two officers returned to the room, solemn expressions on their faces. I sucked in a deep breath of air. I thought they were going to arrest me.

But instead, they said they were letting me go. For now. They were continuing their investigation. Blah blah.

I didn't hear the rest.

I was so happy they were letting me go home.

Mrs. Richards started to sob. Jamie's dad put his arm around her, trying to comfort her.

Jamie's dad helped me to their car. I felt like a limp noodle. I could barely walk. He was really nice to me, very gentle and soothing.

Mrs. Richards sat in the front seat of the car and didn't say a word the whole way home.

That was three nights ago.

Now, I sat in Nights Bar at one-thirty on a Wednesday morning, staring at the yellow neon Budweiser sign behind the bar.

I shared a table with Jamie and Lewis. They had both been so sweet to me ever since Saturday night. I don't think I could have survived without them.

You can imagine the cold stares I got when I returned to school Monday morning. And at Ada's funeral, I could tell that everyone there was accusing me of her murder.

Yes, I went to Ada's funeral. I know it would have been easier to stay home. But I wanted to show everyone I am innocent. I had just as much right as anyone else to go to that funeral.

As we made our way from the church, Aaron, Whitney, and Galen deliberately pushed past me. And I heard Aaron murmur the word "murderer."

Now, the three of them sat in a booth in the back of the bar, staring at me coldly, leaning across the table, talking softly, probably about me.

I tried to ignore them. But I felt uncomfortable and totally tense being near people who thought I could do something that horrible.

I wanted to run to their booth and scream, "Yes, I'm a Fear. But that doesn't mean I'm a killer."

Of course I didn't do that. Instead, I tried to make small talk with Jamie and Lewis.

And then Nate walked into the bar.

He kissed the bronze plaque of the Fears and then stared right at me.

Had I talked to Nate since the night of the skating party? No.

Did he call me to ask how I was feeling? Did he call to say he believed in me, he knew I wasn't the murderer? No.

Did he say a single word to me in school? Three guesses.

My breath caught in my throat as he slowly began walking toward our table. I'd been feeling so hurt all week. Hurt that Nate was like all the rest.

I tried to understand it from his side. Yes, he'd been going with Ada. Yes, he'd cared about her too.

But I thought he had real feeling for me. Isn't that why he invited me to the skating party?

He nodded his head to Jamie and Lewis. Then he took my arm. His dark eyes locked on mine. "Dana, can I talk to you?"

He pulled me to the bar. "Nate, where've you been?" I asked. I couldn't hide my anger.

He shook his head. "In a daze, I guess." He didn't let go of my arm. "I'm sorry, Dana. I wanted to call you, but—"

"But what?" I demanded.

"I stayed home," he said, avoiding my gaze. "I couldn't think about anything. I know I should have called or something. But I didn't call anyone. I was . . . scared."

I pushed his hand away. "Scared of *me*?"

"No," he said quickly. "No way. Just scared. I mean, look. It's frightening, right? Two girls in our class are dead."

"And . . . you think that I—?"

"No," he said again. "I don't know what to think, Dana. I—just—"

"I didn't even know Candy," I said. "She died before I came to Shadyside."

"I know," he said.

"How can anyone suspect me?" I cried. "I'm a good person. I'd never kill anyone."

Nate finally raised his eyes to mine. "I know," he said again. And then he wrapped his arms around me and pulled me close.

For a moment, pressed against him, I felt safe. I held my face against his and hugged him tightly.

Suddenly, I realized we weren't alone. I turned to find Whitney, Aaron, and Galen standing in front of us, cold glares on their faces.

"Oh." I let out a startled cry and let go of Nate.

"We heard what you were saying," Whitney said. "Well, why don't you tell us this? If you'd never kill anyone, Dana, what about your boyfriend back home? Tell us you didn't kill him, too!"

19

My breath caught in my throat. I felt my heart skip a beat.

"Dustin?" I choked out. "You found out about Dustin?"

Whitney stared at me coldly, challenging me, her hands pressed tightly at her waist. She nodded. "I have a friend at your old school. She told me the whole story."

I sank back against the wall. I struggled to catch my breath. "But . . . no one *knows* the whole story."

"I do," Whitney sneered. "You killed him, too."

"That's a LIE!" I screamed. "It was a horrible accident. That's what the police said—and that's the truth."

Whitney, Aaron, and Galen stared at me,

waiting for me to tell them more. Nate put his arm around my shoulder. "Jamie told us you've had a hard year," he said softly. "I didn't know your boyfriend died."

I fought back the tears, but I could feel them running down my cheeks. "It was an accident," I said. "Dustin and I . . . we were hanging out in my pool. In my backyard. It was a beautiful afternoon. I went in the house to make us some sandwiches."

I kept my eyes on Nate as I told the story. I couldn't stand the cold, accusing expressions of the other three kids.

"I wasn't feeling well that day. I had a big fight with my father that morning. It messed me up, made me feel horrible. I . . . I was finishing the sandwiches. I heard a splash outside. And . . . and . . ."

Nate squeezed me gently. "It's okay," he whispered. "You don't have to go on if—"

I took a deep breath and continued. I wanted Whitney and the two boys to know the truth.

"I carried the sandwiches to the pool. I . . . dropped the tray when I saw Dustin. He—he was floating facedown in the pool. And the water around him—it was pink. The tray broke and the sandwiches scattered around me. And I just stared at the pink water.

"It took me so long to realize what made the water pink. It was Dustin's blood. I started shouting his name. I thought maybe it was a joke. Maybe he was trying to scare me. He liked to do that. But, no. He was . . . dead.

"I just stood there, frozen, and watched his body bob in the pink water. I didn't scream or anything. I just stood there, not moving, not breathing. Not believing it, I guess.

"The police decided Dustin had tried a dive and hit his head on the side. It must have knocked him unconscious. His head was cracked open and he drowned."

I used my sleeve to wipe the tears from my face. My whole body was trembling. Nate held me tightly.

I turned to my three accusers. Their cold expressions hadn't changed.

"Good story," Whitney muttered, rolling her eyes.

"Whitney, that was the worst day of my life!" I cried. "I really loved Dustin. How *dare* you accuse me! How can you be so cruel?"

Whitney let out a furious shout. She grabbed my T-shirt with both hands and jerked me close to her. "How can I be so cruel?" she screamed. "How can I be so cruel?"

"Let go of me," I said, struggling to pull her hands away.

"How can I be so cruel?" she repeated, spitting the words in my face. "You killed my best friend—that's how. I know you did."

She tightened her grip on my shirt and jerked me hard, back and forth. Her face was bright red now, and tears flowed down her cheeks.

"You killed my best friend!" she shrieked. You killed Ada—just to get her boyfriend and her scholarship!"

"No!" I cried. "No! Let go of me!"

Jamie and Lewis pushed between Aaron and Galen. Jamie grabbed Whitney around the waist and tried to pull her off me.

"You killed Ada!" Whitney screamed. "You killed her! You killed her! You're a Fear—and that means you're a killer!"

Wailing and sobbing, Whitney started pounding me with her fists. Covering my face, I tried to squirm away.

I heard Ryland shouting.

Someone pulled Whitney away.

I lowered my hands and saw Galen and Aaron holding her, helping her out of the bar. She was sobbing at the top of her lungs, shaking her fists wildly in front of her.

Trembling, my heart racing, I turned to Jamie. "What am I going to do? She's crazy," I whispered. "She'll convince everyone I'm a murderer. How can I stop her?"

20

Friday night I was hunched over my laptop trying to do some homework when Nate IM'd me:

> *Dana, r u there? Can I come see u?*

I was in a bad mood. I messaged him back:

> *Aren't u afraid to be alone with a murderer?*

He ignored my question and wrote:

> *c u soon.*

I jumped up and hurried to change out of the torn T-shirt and baggy jeans I was wearing. I pulled on a bright pink sweater over straight-legged black pants. Very sexy. I pulled a necklace from my dresser drawer and slid it around my neck.

Then I put on lip gloss and brushed my hair.

I kept thinking about Nate, how he held me in the bar, how he hugged me. How he tried to protect me from Whitney's attack.

But a lot of questions nagged at the back of my mind.

What did Nate really think?

He didn't call me for three days after Ada died. Why not? Because he thought I killed Ada?

If not, who did he think was the murderer?

Jamie was standing by me. When Whitney glared at me in the hall at school, Jamie glared right back at her. Lewis believed in me too.

And I wanted Nate to trust me. I really did. I needed someone to rely on, and I hoped that someone was Nate.

The doorbell rang. Jamie and Lewis were at a movie. Danny was staying with a friend. Jamie's parents were out too. I was the only one home.

I ran down the stairs and pulled open the front door.

Nate had a smile on his face. But when he saw me, his eyes went wide and his mouth dropped open.

I realized he was staring at my chest. "Nate? What's wrong?" I asked.

"That pendant," he said, pointing. "Where did you get it?"

My hand went to the necklace. "I made it," I said. "Why? What's wrong with it?"

He didn't answer. He grabbed it gently and smoothed his hand over it. The pendant was made of silver wire with blue glass cut to look like jewels.

"It's not old?" he asked finally. He let go of it and took a step back.

"No. I told you. I made it," I said.

It was a cold, blustery kind of night, black storm clouds low in the sky. Nate stood there with his denim jacket open, a black T-shirt underneath. "Aren't you cold?" I said.

I stepped aside and motioned for Nate to come into the house. I closed the door behind him. He was still studying the pendant.

"It just looks old," I said. "I copied the design from old photos of Angelica Fear."

He swallowed. "You did? You have photos of Angelica Fear?"

I nodded. "Well, yes. I told you I've studied the history of the Fears. It *is* my family, after all." I tugged his arm. "Want to see the photos of her?"

"For sure," he said.

I led him up to my room in the attic. He looked around, ducking his head under the slanting ceiling. "Cozy," he said. He grabbed my arms and tried to pull me on top of him on the bed.

"Hey, I thought you wanted to see old photos," I said.

He kissed me. We kissed for a while. I held the sides of his face, held him there, needing him, needing someone to care about me.

Then, breathless, I pulled away and dropped down to my file drawer. He sat on the bed and watched me as I searched for the Angelica Fear photos.

"Here." I handed both of them to him. "The date on the back says eighteen ninety-five. They're pretty faded. I had to tape that one back together. It kinda crumbled."

He studied the first photo for a long time, then moved to the second one. "That's the amulet," he murmured.

"Do you know about it?" I asked.

He didn't answer. Just stared from one photo to the other.

"Angelica Fear was obsessed with immortality," I said. "I read a lot about her. She was one of the most interesting Fears—and one of the most evil. She was into all kinds of witch-craft and sorcery. She did a lot of experi-ments, trying to bring dead people back to life. She said she would live forever. She told people she had found the secret."

Nate finally put down the photos. He gazed at me. I didn't know if he'd heard a word I said. "Why did you copy her amulet?" he asked.

I shrugged. "I just thought it was kinda cool. You know. Mysterious looking. I was really into jewelry-making for a while. Jamie isn't the only artistic one in the family."

He turned back to the amulet. "Did Angelica wear it because it had magical pow-ers? Was that her secret for living forever?"

I shrugged. "Beats me. Maybe she thought it had powers. I didn't read about that any-where."

I turned the amulet over in my hand. "Do you believe in that supernatural stuff, Nate?"

He snickered. A strange smile spread over his face. "I may know more about the amulet than you do, Dana," he said.

I stared at him. "Excuse me? What are you talking about?"

He let out a sigh and leaned back on my bed. "Can I trust you? I've been dying to tell this to someone."

"Of course you can," I said. I dropped down beside him on the bed and took his hand. "What's wrong, Nate? What is it?"

"This is a secret," he said, lowering his voice. "I know how Candy died. I mean, I was there. It was because of this amulet."

I grabbed the amulet. "Not *this* one."

"No," he said. "Another copy of it. A plastic copy of it. Candy wore it all the time. Shark and I—we didn't know it was plastic. We thought it was really Angelica Fear's amulet. And we thought Candy was using it to put a curse on us."

I squeezed his hand. "A curse? You mean the cockroaches? The blood spurting from your ears?"

He nodded. "There's more. One day my car drove into the river with four of us inside it. We almost drowned."

I shook my head. "Wow. And you thought Candy . . ."

"Yes. We thought Candy was doing it. You've got to swear not to tell anyone, Dana. I've had this secret inside me for weeks. Late one night, Shark, Nikki, and I sneaked into Candy's house. We knew she was all alone. We wanted to steal the amulet. But . . ."

"But what happened?" I asked.

"We took it from her room. But she woke up. She tried to grab it back. And . . . and she fell down the stairs. She broke her neck. She was dead. We knew she was dead. And we just ran. And then . . . then we found out her amulet was a fake. Just like yours."

I stared at him and held on to his hand. I could see the horror on his face. I hoped it had helped him to tell the story to someone.

"We never told anyone we were there that night when Candy died," he said. "But here's the weird part. Later, I went to bed—and I found a pig's head in my bed. A bloody pig's head under my covers."

I gasped. "But—how? What does that mean?"

He lowered his voice to a whisper. "It means there's something evil out there. I don't know why. I can just feel it, Dana."

He grabbed me and held on to me. "I know you didn't kill Ada. But someone did. And . . . and Candy didn't just fall. She went *flying*. It wasn't natural. It was like an invisible force pushed her."

"An invisible force?" I said, my voice trembling. "Evil? You really believe that?"

He nodded.

I hugged him and held him tightly. He was so tense, I could almost feel the fear in his body.

"Something evil out there . . ." As I pressed my cheek against his, the words repeated in my mind.

Impossible, I thought. Impossible.

But, Monday afternoon, I started to agree with him.

21

Four folding chairs were lined up in a row in front of the curtain on the auditorium stage. I stared at the four chairs as I walked down the aisle, and my throat tightened.

I can't sing today, I thought. I'm too nervous.

Get it together, Dana, I scolded myself. I had no choice. I had to sing. This afternoon was the first round in the singing competition for the Collingsworth Prize.

I saw ten or twelve kids hunched in seats near the stage. Jamie waved to me. She and Lewis had come to cheer me on.

At the side, Ms. Watson sat with three other teachers. They all had clipboards in their laps. They were the judges. I waved to Ms. Watson, and she smiled back.

My throat felt even tighter. I struggled to swallow. My mouth suddenly felt as if it were filled with sand.

How can I do this?

I felt a hand tap me on the shoulder. Startled, I jumped.

Nate grinned at me. "Sorry. A little tense?"

"You got that right," I said. "Are you staying for the contest?"

He nodded. "I'm going to send you good vibes. Who else is singing? Whitney, right?"

The sound of her name sent a shiver down my back. "Yeah, Whitney," I said. "And Sharona and Yuri."

Nate's eyes went wide. "Yuri? He's a math nerd. I didn't know he could sing."

"Jamie says Yuri can do everything," I replied.

Nate squeezed my shoulder. "Don't worry about him. You're gonna win this thing. It's a piece of cake. I know it."

"I *need* to win it," I said. "If I don't, my life is garbage." I realized I was squeezing the amulet, almost tugging it off its chain.

Nate kissed me on the cheek. "Go get 'em."

I glanced up to the stage. Whitney had already taken her seat at the end of the row of folding chairs. She looked very prim in a loose, white top and a knee-length gray skirt. She was straightening her long, blond hair with one hand.

When she saw me, her smile faded. Her face went hard. She glared at me and mouthed a word.

I recognized it: MURDERER.

"Whitney hates me so much," I whispered to Nate. "Check out that look on her face."

Nate raised his eyes to the stage. "Cold," he murmured.

"Jamie tried to reason with her," I said, holding on to his arm. But Whitney wouldn't listen." I sighed. "Jamie and Whitney were good friends—before I showed up."

Nate gripped my shoulders. "Hey, forget all that," he said. "Don't think about Whitney. Just get up there and sing."

I nodded. "You're right. Thanks, Nate."

I followed Yuri and Sharona onto the stage. I took the chair at the far end, as far away from Whitney as I could get.

I hoped I didn't have to sing first. I needed

time to get my head together. But wouldn't you know it? Ms. Watson motioned for me to step to the microphone.

I handed her my music and tried to clear my throat, taking deep breaths as she walked to the piano. I knew Whitney was sending me hate vibes. I looked straight out at the kids in the audience.

I sang "Mister Snow," from the Broadway musical *Carousel*. I probably should have done something classical. But I knew this was my best song.

I did okay. Not my best performance. My voice was a little thin in the beginning. I could hear it, but I hoped maybe the judges didn't notice.

When I finished, Jamie, Nate, and Lewis went wild, cheering and shouting. The other kids clapped politely.

As I took my seat, I glanced at the judges. They were scribbling furiously on their clip-boards. One of them had a smile on her face. The other two had blank expressions.

I turned and saw Whitney striding over to Ms. Watson at the piano. She handed her some sheet music, then stepped up to the microphone, tugging her top down over her skirt.

I shut my eyes. I suddenly felt kinda strange. Dizzy. A little faint.

Just tension, I told myself.

Whitney announced that she was singing a number by Dvořák. She cleared her throat noisily. Ms. Watson started to play.

Whitney opened her mouth to sing—but stopped.

She sneezed.

Ms. Watson stopped playing. She turned to Whitney. "Ready now?"

Whitney raised a hand, signaling for Ms. Watson to wait. She sneezed again. Then again. Loud, violent sneezes.

Whitney's eyes bulged. "Aaaack!" Whitney let out a cry. She reached up to her nose and started to pull something out. Something slender and white.

At first, I thought it was a Kleenex or a handkerchief. But then I realized Whitney had pulled a *feather* from her nose.

Some kids giggled. I heard a few gasps.

Whitney held the feather in two fingers, staring at it in bewilderment.

"Whitney, are you okay?" Ms. Watson called from the piano.

Whitney didn't reply. She sneezed again. "Ohhhhh." A low groan escaped her throat. Slowly, very slowly, she pulled another long, white feather from her nose.

This time, no one laughed. The auditorium grew very quiet.

"Aaaack. Oh, help!"

Whitney tugged another long feather from her nose. As soon as it was in her hand, another feather poked out. She pulled it out quickly, and another feather appeared.

"NOOOOOOOO!" Whitney opened her mouth in a scream of horror.

Still feeling dizzy and faint, I gripped my pendant and watched the slender, white feathers float to the stage floor at her feet.

Feather after feather slid out. And then the auditorium erupted in screams as the feathers came out bright red. Blood started to flow from her nose.

Whitney sneezed hard. Again. Again.

She screamed and pulled out another blood-soaked feather.

"Help me! Somebody—HELP me!"

The feathers piled at her feet, and the glistening, red blood poured onto the feathers.

The blood ran down the front of her white blouse. Another dripping, red feather slid from her nose.

Whitney spun around and shook a finger at me. "DANA is doing this!" she shrieked. "She's using her Fear powers! She's doing this to me!"

Lots of gasps and startled cries in the audience. The three judges were on their feet, their faces tight with horror.

Whitney covered her face, but the blood continued to flow, pouring from her nose, puddling at her already blood-soaked shoes.

22

"Dana, my mom's very worried about you," Jamie said, poking her head into my room. "You didn't come down to dinner."

I was sprawled on my back in bed, reading an old copy of *People* magazine. I dropped the magazine to my side. "I'm just not hungry," I said. "Tell her I'll grab something later."

Jamie crossed the room, stepping over the dirty clothing I'd tossed in a pile. She sat down on the edge of the bed. "You've been moping around for three days. You've been acting so weird. Ever since . . ."

I pulled myself up to a sitting position. I felt my stomach churning. Every muscle in my body was tense and knotted. "Of *course* I've been acting weird. I'm like a freak at school!" I cried.

Jamie narrowed her eyes at me. I could see she was surprised by my outburst.

"Ever since the thing with Whitney," I continued, unable to keep my voice steady. "No one is talking to me, Jamie. I'm a total outcast. I say hi to people, and they cut me dead. They don't even look at me."

"But, Dana—," Jamie started.

"Everyone thinks I made the feathers come out of Whitney's nose. Because I'm a Fear, everyone thinks I used magic to keep Whitney from singing. But that's CRAZY!"

I was screaming now, my voice so high that even dogs couldn't hear it. Jamie tried to take my hand, but I jerked it away.

"I don't know any magic!" I cried. "And I wouldn't do that to Whitney. My name is Fear, but I'm not evil. I don't know any tricks at all. How could I make feathers appear in Whitney's nose? No way! How can anyone even *think* I could do it?"

Jamie stood up. She bit her bottom lip, studying me.

I had tears in my eyes. Angry tears. I wiped them away before they could slide down my cheeks.

"Can I give you one piece of advice?" Jamie asked, speaking softly.

I nodded.

"Don't wear that amulet to school. I know you made it and everything. But a lot of kids are afraid of it."

"Huh? Okay," I said. I ripped it off my neck and tossed it in the trash.

I sneaked out of the house a little after one in the morning and made my way to Nights Bar on Fear Street.

I wasn't going to go. I didn't want more kids staring at me—those cold, accusing stares. I knew I couldn't take it much longer.

I'd gone to bed early. I wrapped myself up in a tiny ball, hugging my pillow like a teddy bear, and tried to sleep.

But Nate called on my cell and begged me to come to the bar. He said he really wanted to talk to me.

So here I was. In a worn sweater and an old pair of jeans, torn at the knees. Did I stop to brush my hair? I couldn't even remember.

A cool, clear night. Lots of stars twinkling

in the sky. No one else around, of course. The town asleep, except for us.

I waved to Ryland O'Connor and purposely didn't kiss the bronze plaque of Simon and Angelica Fear. Then Nate pulled me to a booth at the back wall. The bar was crowded with kids. But they were a blur to me. I kept my eyes straight ahead. I didn't care who was there.

I dropped into the booth, and Nate squeezed beside me. He kissed me. He'd been really nice to me ever since that frightening afternoon in the auditorium.

"I . . . didn't want to come out tonight," I said. "But when you called . . ."

He started to unzip my parka. "Are you wearing the amulet?"

"Excuse me?" I moved his hands away. "No. I threw it in the trash."

He squinted at me. "Really? Well, I found out more about it. The real one, I mean."

Ryland came up to the table. Nate ordered a beer. I asked for coffee.

"You did research on it?" I asked.

"Yeah. On the Net," he said. "I found some interesting Web sites."

I pulled off my parka and stuffed it on the other side of the booth. Then I snuggled next to Nate. "What did you learn about the amulet? That it makes feathers fly out of people's noses?"

He shook his head. "Forget about feathers, Dana. Angelica Fear was convinced she could use the amulet to come back from the grave. And—"

"We already know that," I interrupted.

"She believed she could come back from the grave *and inhabit a living person's body,*" Nate said.

I stared at him. "So?"

"Don't you see?" Nate slapped the table-top. "Who else could be doing all these horrible things? It can't be any of us. We're all just trying to slog through high school, right? We're not murderers or sorcerers. We just want to get through senior year and party a little and have some fun."

"I guess . . . ," I said. I didn't really understand where he was going with this.

"So, I've been thinking," Nate continued. "Thinking a lot. I mean, they tore down the old Fear Mansion last year, right? It was on this spot where we're sitting. And they tore down all the other Fear Street houses to put up the shopping center."

"Yeah. Right," I said.

"Well, what if Angelica Fear was buried under the mansion or something?" Nate asked, eyes wide with excitement. "What if her grave was disturbed when they dug up the old place? What if a lot of graves were disturbed, and the ghosts of Fear Street all escaped from them?"

"Nate, please—," I started.

He squeezed my wrist. "Dana, listen. What if Angelica really *did* know how to come back to life? What if she came back to life last year with all her evil tricks and is living inside someone's body. Someone we know!"

"STOP!" I screamed. "I mean it, Nate. Stop! Don't you realize how crazy that sounds?"

His face fell. He looked hurt. "Of course it sounds crazy," he said. "But look at all the crazy things that have been happening. How do you explain—?"

"You've been hanging out with my cousin Jamie too long," I said. "Jamie believes in all that supernatural stuff."

Nate opened his mouth to say something,

but he never got it out. Shark appeared at the table, with Nikki close behind him.

Shark had a black leather jacket open over a black T-shirt, collar up, over black denims. He had a black wool ski cap pulled down over his hair. Nikki's white-blond hair hung wildly about her face. She wore a pale green parka, and brown corduroy pants tucked into furry Ugg boots.

Shark grabbed Nate's shoulder. "Yo, dude. What's up?"

"I'm talking about evil ghosts," Nate said. "Doing evil things to our friends."

"Shut *up*! Are you freaked about Whitney?" Nikki asked. "Shark told me about it, and—"

"Do we have to talk about that stuff?" Shark asked. "Hey, we used to sneak out late at night for *fun*—remember? We're the Night People. We stay up all night. So why aren't we having fun anymore?"

Nate finished his beer. He slammed the bottle on the tabletop. "Yeah. Let's do it. Shark is right. Come on, Dana. Let's go out and just goof around. Like we used to."

The four of us left the bar and stepped out into the cool, still night. The Fear Street Acres shopping center stood across the street from Nights. The stores were dimly lit, the doors and windows barred and locked.

We walked along the shops, peering into windows, joking about the junk we saw, goofing on one another. Shark overturned a few trash cans, just because he could, I guess.

The noise must have awakened a dark-uniformed security guard, who poked his head around the wall of a building. We quickly darted into a store entrance.

I held my breath, listening for his footsteps. But he didn't come after us.

Shark snickered. "Are we having fun yet?"

I held on to Nate as we made our way out of the shopping center. Clouds rolled over the moon. A cold wind ruffled my hair.

We stopped and kissed. The kiss lasted a long time. We had to run to catch up to Nikki and Shark.

A few minutes later, we found ourselves outside the Fear Street Cemetery. Tangled trees formed a wall along the sidewalk. Behind them, I could see ragged rows of low gravestones poking up at strange angles.

The wind whispered through the trees,

shaking the bare limbs, like in a bad horror movie.

"You're supposed to hold your breath when you pass a graveyard," Shark said.

"What happens if you don't?" Nikki asked.

He grinned at her. "Feathers come out of your nose."

Shark and Nate laughed. Nikki gave Shark a hard shove that sent him staggering into a fat tree trunk.

"I thought we weren't going to talk about that," I said.

I turned to Nate. He had his eyes on a tall tree a few feet ahead of us. "Hey, Nate—?" I called. I reached for him, but he ducked away.

I saw the look of horror spread over his face. "Look OUT!" he screamed. "It's the one-eyed bird!"

I squinted up into the tree. I couldn't see it. "Where?" I cried.

Nate pointed frantically to a tree limb. Then he darted to one side. Off-balance, he fell to the grass. "Look out! It's attacking!" he screamed.

He dropped to his knees and raised his arms to shield his face. "Run! It's attacking! *Run!*"

23

My breath caught in my throat. I heard a fluttering sound.

The flap of wings?

No. Dead leaves blown by the wind.

Shark laughed. He pulled Nate to his feet. "You're joking, right?" he said.

His face knotted with terror, Nate searched the treetops. "The bird—"

"What's your problem?" Shark asked him. "None of us saw any bird. It was probably leaves falling or something."

I took Nate's arm. He was trembling, breathing hard. "I saw it," he insisted. "It came swooping down at me."

"Whoa. Creepy," Nikki said.

Shark grinned. He turned to me. "How many beers did Nate have tonight?"

"No. I saw it," Nate repeated. "I saw the blackbird." He shook his head. "What's *happening* to me?"

Nate said to meet him in the gym after school on Monday. I wasn't feeling great. I had a throbbing headache, and I'd been feeling dizzy and kinda weak again.

Just nerves, I hoped.

The thud of a basketball on the gym floor made my head pound. Some kids were having a relaxed game of basketball. I recognized Nate and Yuri and Shark and some girls from my class.

And then I saw Whitney. The others were laughing and kidding around. But she had this intense expression on her face. I watched her dribble up to Shark, fake him out, and go in to score with a driving layup.

Whitney is on the varsity girls' team, I remembered.

I turned to leave, but Nate came running over. "Hey, Dana. How's it going? Go get some sneakers on. Join us."

"I don't think so," I said. "I'm not feeling great, and—"

No way I'd join a game with Whitney on the court.

What was Nate thinking?

"Hey, come on—get in the game!" Shark shouted, waving to me. "We're going to play shirts and skins. The girls are going to be the skins!"

Some kids actually laughed at that.

"I'm feeling kinda weird," I told Nate. "I'll wait for you over there." I pointed to the bleachers.

I took a seat in the second row. I rubbed my forehead with my fingers, trying to rub the ache away. I had my eyes closed. I listened to the *thud thud thud* of the ball and the scrape of sneakers over the floor.

I heard a shout and opened my eyes—in time for the ball to smash me in the chest.

"Hey—" I uttered a shocked cry. Pain shot through my body.

"Oh. Sorry," Whitney said in this fake tone. "It got away from me."

I knew she deliberately heaved it at me. I wanted to jump up and strangle her!

"I'm okay," I said.

Shark picked up the ball and tossed it downcourt to Yuri. The game started up again.

Whitney was the best player on the floor. She seemed to be beating everyone single-handedly.

After a while, I heard someone shouting my name. I turned to the gym doors and saw Jamie waving at me. "I'm going to my pottery class," she shouted. "See you later!"

I waved to her. When I turned back, the game was breaking up. "Dana—I'll be right out," Nate called. He followed Shark and Yuri to the locker room to get changed.

The girls were trotting off the court too. "Whitney, are you coming?" one of them called.

"In a few minutes," Whitney shouted back. "I keep messing up these jump shots."

Whitney and I were alone in the gym now. I leaned back against the bleacher and watched her do jump shot after jump shot. She never looked my way. She was totally intent on getting her jump shots right.

I suddenly felt a wave of nausea roll down my body. I blinked, feeling dizzy. I felt my heart jump in my chest.

Why do I feel so weird? I wondered.

I shut my eyes. I rested my head in my hands, waiting for the strange feeling to pass by.

Everything went gray. Like a thick fog.

Did I pass out? I don't know.

The next thing I knew, Nate was shaking me hard by the shoulders. "Dana? Dana?" He kept repeating my name in a high, tense voice.

I opened my eyes. I shook my head, trying to clear it.

"Nate? What's wrong?"

He turned. It took a while for my eyes to focus. When they finally did, I saw a girl. Lying on her back on the gym floor, arms and legs outstretched.

"Ohh." I uttered a low moan. I recognized Whitney's bright red sneakers.

And then I saw the blood. A bright red puddle spreading over the floor at her shoulders. Her shoulders . . . her neck . . .

I jumped to my feet. My legs trembled. My breath caught in my throat. "Nate—?" I gasped.

I stared at the headless body on the floor. And then I raised my eyes and saw the head—blond hair falling over her face . . . I saw the head up in the basket.

Whitney's head staring blankly down at me from the bloodstained net.

PART FOUR

PART FOUR

24

I had no one I could talk to after that. Even Nate sounded different when I talked to him.

I called his cell late Wednesday night. I didn't want to go to Nights, but I couldn't bear to be alone, either. "I just need to talk," I told Nate.

"You kinda woke me up," he said.

"I don't care," I snapped. I was in bed with the blankets pulled up over my head. But I still didn't feel safe. "You have no idea what my life has been like," I said.

I heard Nate yawn. "Listen, Dana—"

"Thank God Jamie's dad is a lawyer," I said. "He's been so wonderful. He sat in while the police questioned me. He took care of everything."

"Great," Nate said sleepily. "That was lucky."

"I called my own dad," I continued. "I told him I was in major trouble. Know what he said? He said he was on a big business trip and couldn't make it. Do you believe that?"

"Weird," Nate replied.

What was with the one-word answers? Was he deliberately acting cold to me?

He couldn't believe I killed Whitney— *could* he?

I didn't care. I had to talk to someone. I had to let it all out.

"The police were tough," I continued, squeezing my cell against my ear. "They think they see a pattern. So far, two girls competing for the Collingsworth Prize have been killed: Ada and Whitney. They know how desperate I am to win that prize. So . . . I have a motive. A motive for killing those two."

"Oh, wow," Nate murmured.

"I don't think they believed me about my blackouts. About how dizzy and faint I felt. How I kinda passed out and everything went gray. They're checking with my doctor back home. But it *never* happened to me back home!"

I took a deep breath. My heart was hammering in my chest. "Sure, the prize means a lot to me," I told Nate. "But I'm not a killer. And I'll tell you one thing the police never mentioned."

"What's that?" Nate asked.

"If someone is killing all the Collingsworth contestants, I could be next. Don't you see? I could be the next victim!"

"Don't think like that," Nate said. "You'll be okay."

I was shivering under the blankets. Nate sounded so cold and insincere. I suddenly felt terrified—and totally alone.

"I've got to catch some sleep," he said, yawning.

"Bye," I said, and clicked off the phone.

I stifled a sob. Was he just tired, or was he like all the others? They all believed I killed those girls.

Was it possible?

Could I have murdered them while I was in that gray fog? Could I be guilty and have no memory of what I'd done?

No. No way. I wouldn't let myself think that way. Not for a moment.

I dropped my cell phone to the floor. Nate's cold, uninterested voice lingered in my ears. I sat up and shoved the blankets away.

I knew I couldn't sleep. I had to talk to someone, someone who believed in me.

Jamie.

When I came home from the police station Monday night, she threw her arms around me and hugged me. I could feel the hot tears on her cheeks.

"I know you didn't do it," she whispered. "I know you didn't. I'll stick by you, Dana. No matter what happens next."

Yes, Jamie seemed to be my last remaining friend. I hoped she hadn't sneaked out to Nights. I really needed her tonight.

I climbed out of bed and straightened my nightshirt. I pushed back my hair. Then I tiptoed down the attic stairs and across the hall to Jamie's room.

Was she in there? Her bedroom door was open just a crack. From the hall I could see flickering light inside the room.

I pushed the door open a little more. And realized I was peering into candlelight. Light and shadows danced and darted around the room.

I poked my head in. To my surprise, I saw Jamie down on her knees on the floor. She knelt in a circle of black candles. She had her back to me. I could see her hair, black in the flickering candlelight, flowing wildly behind her head.

What was she doing down there?

I held my breath and listened. She had her head down. She was reciting something, chanting words I didn't recognize. Her voice was soft and low, rising and falling in a strange melody.

I listened, not moving, not breathing.

What language was that?

A chill ran down my back. I grasped the door handle.

Squinting into the orange light, I saw little bowls on the floor. Chanting softly, Jamie bent over them. She lifted a bowl and poured a dark powder into another bowl.

I watched her sift the powder with her fingers. She poured the powder from bowl to bowl, bending low, chanting in that strange, musical language.

I wanted to call out to her. But I didn't dare interrupt.

And then she turned. And I saw her face.

Gripping the door, I stared wide-eyed at her face, flickering in the orange light.

But it wasn't her face.

Older eyes. A turned-up nose. An aged, ragged, half-smile.

Definitely not Jamie's face!

25

I ducked back. I didn't want her to see me.

I'm imagining this, I decided. It's just the darkness, the shadows falling over the orange light.

No. I could see the face clearly. A woman's face—not Jamie's face.

My heart fluttering in my chest, I turned and stumbled to the stairs. I pulled myself up to my room, dove into bed, and tugged the covers to my chin.

Impossible, I thought. Impossible. *Impossible.* I kept repeating the word in my mind.

But the picture of that face—the *other face*—wouldn't go away.

My brain whirred. I struggled to make

sense of what I saw. But I couldn't explain it. I didn't have a clue.

Did she see me? Did Jamie see me watching her from the doorway?

Another shiver rolled down my back. I struggled to catch my breath, to slow my racing heartbeats.

And then I heard a sound. A soft creak. The creak of the attic stairs.

I sucked in a deep breath and held it. And listened.

Yes. Footsteps on the attic stairs. Another creak.

In the dim, gray light from the hall, I saw Jamie creep into my room. Her face was hidden in shadow. I pretended to be asleep but kept my eyes open just a crack, open enough to watch her.

She hesitated in the doorway. Stood perfectly still. Making sure I wasn't awake, I guessed.

Then she made her way to the couch. I had my school clothes there, laid out for tomorrow morning. A skirt, long-sleeved top, tights.

I lifted my head off the pillow to see better.

Jamie carried something in her hand. Squinting hard, I recognized one of the small bowls. I watched her reach into the bowl. She began to sprinkle powder over my clothes. And as her fingers moved back and forth, she chanted softly, murmuring words in that strange language.

What was she chanting? What was she *doing*?

An ancient spell?

I couldn't breathe. I couldn't move.

I watched in icy horror as my cousin emptied the bowl of powder over my clothes. And I listened to her strange, soft song in that raspy, whispered voice.

Not her voice. Not Jamie's voice at all.

Staring in horrified disbelief, I squeezed the edge of the blanket till my hands ached. And when she finally tiptoed from the room, I sat up with one thought in my mind:

I've got to get out of this house!

26

I waited until I was sure Jamie had gone downstairs. Then I crept across the room and clicked my bedroom door shut.

My hand trembled as I grabbed my cell phone off the floor. And pushed in a number. "Dad, it's me," I whispered.

"Huh? Dana? You woke me up. What time is it?"

"Dad, I know it's the middle of the night. But you have to come get me. Now."

"Dana? What? What are you saying?"

"You've got to take me away from here," I pleaded. "There's something *sick* going on. And—"

"Dana, are you high on something? Are you drunk? Why are you calling me so late?"

"Just listen to me, Dad. Please. For once.

Just listen to me. I need you to listen. It's Jamie. She—"

"What about Jamie? Speak up. I can barely hear you."

"I can't speak up. She'll hear me. Dad, I'm frightened. Seriously frightened. Jamie is using some kind of magic. I don't know what she's up to. I saw her sprinkle my clothes with powder. I think she's trying to poison me or something. Dad—"

"Dana, you're talking crazy," he said. "Listen to what you're saying. You're not making sense. Have you been drinking?"

"I know it sounds crazy, but it isn't," I insisted, my voice breaking with emotion. "You've *got* to believe me. She's doing something to me and—"

"Calm down. Just calm down. Take a breath, okay? Get some sleep, Dana. You'll feel a lot better in the morning."

"No. You've *got* to come get me, Dad."

"Look. I'm in Atlanta. I can't just drop everything."

"Dad, please—"

"Tell you what. I'll try to come next weekend. I think I can clear my schedule. But get yourself together. I mean it. You're talking like a crazy person."

"Dad——?"

He hung up.

I didn't sleep all night. I thought about packing up my stuff and running away. But where could I go?

In the morning, I left the skirt and top on the couch. I put on a different outfit, a loose-fitting black turtleneck over green cords. I grabbed my backpack and crept downstairs.

I heard voices in the kitchen. I poked my head through the doorway. Jamie sat at the kitchen table, finishing a bowl of cereal. Her mom stood at the kitchen counter, a white mug of coffee in her hand.

"No breakfast for me," I said. "I'm going right to school."

"No. I'm sorry," Aunt Audra said. When she turned to me, I saw that her eyes were brimming with tears. "I'm sorry, Dana. I can't let you go to school."

My mouth dropped open. "Excuse me?"

Jamie set down her cereal bowl. She glared at me icily.

"I'm taking you to a doctor," Aunt Audra said. "Before she died, I promised your mother I'd take good care of you, Dana. And now I'm going to see that you get the help you need."

"Huh? Help?"

What was she talking about?

"Your father called me early this morning," she said. "He's very worried about you too."

My heart leaped to my throat. My knees started to buckle. I grabbed the door frame to keep myself up.

Jamie's eyes burned into mine. Her jaw was set tight. She spoke through clenched teeth. "Why did you say those horrible things about me to your dad, Dana?"

"Jamie, listen—"

"I've been so nice to you," she said. "Why did you tell him I'm trying to poison you?" Jamie's eyes grew colder. She raised her butter knife in her fist.

"I'm terribly hurt," she said. "You shouldn't have done that, Dana. You really shouldn't have. . . ."

27

With a gasp, I dropped the backpack, spun away, and started for the stairs.

"Don't go far," Aunt Audra called. "I'm calling Dr. Wilbur as soon as his office opens."

I hurtled up to my room and slammed the door behind me. I paced furiously back and forth in the tiny room, trying to decide on a plan.

What should I do?

After a few minutes I heard the front door slam. From my tiny attic window I saw Jamie trotting toward school, backpack bouncing on her back.

I waited till she was out of sight. Then I took a deep breath, trying to force my heart to stop pounding, and sneaked downstairs to her bedroom.

Her nightshirt was tossed over the bed. A pile of jeans littered the floor in front of the closet. The black candles had been removed. I saw spots of black candle wax on the carpet.

I glanced around. Shoved to the other side of the bed, I saw the big spell book. The old book we had used to try to call up Cindy from the grave.

The book was open to two pages of tiny type. I dropped down to the floor and raised the book to my lap.

I squinted at the narrow columns of type, trying to find what Jamie had been chanting last night. It didn't take long. At the top of the right-hand page, I found what I was looking for.

A spell to fog a person's mind.

I ran a trembling finger over the ancient words.

Yes. A spell to make a person feel faint. To make their minds go blank.

Had Jamie been using this spell on me?

A hundred thoughts shot through my mind at once—all of them horrifying. I pieced together an insane story—just crazy enough to be true.

Jamie used the spell on me to make me go faint. Then she murdered those two girls. She made it look as if I was the murderer. And I was left with no excuse, except that I'd blacked out.

Why?

That was the unanswered question. Why kill her own friends? Why try to put the blame on me? Why would Jamie do that?

A big piece of the puzzle was missing. But I was too terrified to stick around and find it.

I slammed the book shut and jumped to my feet. I had to get out of the house. Had to find someone who would believe me, who would help me.

I stepped out into the hall.

"Dana?" I heard Aunt Audra call from downstairs. "I reached Dr. Wilbur. I'm driving you there in half an hour. Why don't you come down and have some breakfast?"

No! No way.

I pulled on my parka and sneaked out the front door. I took off running, down the driveway and then along the sidewalk. I crossed the street and kept running.

Gasping for breath, my chest aching, I

stopped a few blocks later. I realized where I was running. I was running to Nate's house. He was the only one who could help me. He *had* to help me.

I knocked on his front door and waited. No answer. I rang the bell. No one. I peeked into the front window but couldn't see anyone. The garage door was open. The car was gone.

He must be on his way to school, I decided. So I took off once again, running hard, not thinking, unable to think about anything but finding Nate and begging him to help me escape.

A few minutes later I spotted him in the student parking lot behind the high school. He was climbing out of his mother's blue Accord.

"Thank goodness!" I cried breathlessly.

But then I saw that he wasn't alone. Standing between two cars, he was talking to someone.

I moved closer, keeping low, hiding behind the parked cars. And I recognized Jamie. She was shaking her head, wiping away tears.

I knew she was telling him about me.

Nate slid his arm around Jamie's shoulders. I could see he was comforting her. And then I heard him say, "Dana trusts me. Maybe I can trick her or something. You know. Help get her to the mental hospital."

28

Around four o'clock that afternoon,
I saw Jamie lift the garage door and disappear
into her sculpture studio. The door slid down
noisily behind her.

I watched from the side of the garden shed.
I'd wandered aimlessly all day, trying to make a
plan. Trying to decide what to do, where to go.
Trying to make sense of everything.

I'm not crazy.

I told myself that a hundred times. I don't
belong in a mental hospital. I didn't imagine
the spellbook. And I didn't imagine Jamie
sneaking into my room and spreading powder
on my clothes.

Because of my dear cousin, everyone
thought I was a murderer. And everyone
thought I was insane. And Aunt Audra and my

father probably planned to lock me away in some kind of hospital.

I realized I had no choice. I had to confront Jamie. I had to force her to tell me the truth. And so I waited in the cold, waited by the side of the shed. Waited till she went into her studio.

And now, I took a deep breath and stepped up to the garage door. I slid it open slowly, as quietly as possible, hoping to surprise her.

A blast of warm air greeted me. Jamie had her back to me. She stood at the open door of a huge, flaming pottery kiln, as big as a furnace. I watched her lean toward the kiln, lowering a piece of pottery into the blazing heat.

I let go of the garage door and took a few steps into the studio. A long, well-lit worktable filled the center of the room. A potter's wheel stood at the far end. I glimpsed shelves of red clay pottery—vases and bowls and heads and—

Whoa.

My eyes stopped at the pedestals in front of the worktable. Slender, stone pedestals holding three sculpted heads.

Heads of girls . . .

"Ohhh." I raised my hands to my mouth to stifle the sound of my shocked cry.

I recognized two of the clay heads: Ada and Whitney. Was the third head Candy?

Did Jamie sculpt all three dead girls? And paint them to look so lifelike?

I looked to the back wall. Jamie was still leaning into the open kiln.

I couldn't take my eyes off the sculpted heads. I moved as if in a daze. Hardly realizing what I was doing, I crept up to the pedestals. I reached out a trembling hand. I touched the sculpture of Ada. Touched her cheek.

And opened my mouth in a wail of horror.

The heads . . . they weren't clay. They weren't sculpted.

These were the real heads of the murdered girls!

29

Jamie spun away from the kiln at the sound of my scream. Her eyes went wide with surprise, then narrowed at me coldly.

She moved quickly to the worktable. She picked up a black remote controller and clicked it twice. Behind me, I heard the garage door sliding shut.

"You're locked in," Jamie said, tossing down the controller and moving toward me. "I see you are admiring my art gallery."

"Jamie . . . I—I . . . *why*?" I stammered.

The eyes of the three dead girls stared at me blankly.

"Pretty heads, aren't they?" Jamie said. "And look, Dana—I have an empty pedestal. Whose head do you think should go on it? Yours, maybe?"

I took a step back. I glanced frantically around the garage. No side door. The window was open, but too small to fit through. No way to escape.

I turned back to my cousin. "What have you *done*?" I cried. "Why are these heads—"

My breath caught in my throat.

As I gaped at her, Jamie's face changed. Her eyes darkened. Her cheeks sagged. Her features transformed until she wasn't Jamie anymore.

I realized I was staring at the face I'd seen late last night in Jamie's room. An older woman's face, with icy black eyes and a cruel, tight-lipped smile.

"Jamie isn't here," she said in a dry whisper. "Don't you recognize me, Dana? Don't you know who I am?"

And in that instant, I did recognize her. I recognized her from the photos in my file.

Angelica Fear.

A chill tightened the back of my neck. I stood staring at her, frozen in horror. "I . . . don't understand," I choked out. "How . . . ? Where is Jamie?"

She shrugged. "A year ago, Jamie fell onto my grave in front of the Fear Mansion. So lucky for me. I always knew I could come back to life. I could be immortal."

I pointed. "You . . . you . . ." My teeth were chattering. I couldn't talk.

"I took her body," she said in her low, hoarse whisper. "I'm alive again after a hundred years!"

She reached under her collar and pulled out a jeweled pendant. The amulet! "I have the real one, Dana," she whispered. "The one that has made me immortal." She waved it in front of my face.

"But . . . you killed these girls!" I finally found my voice. Anger was quickly overtaking my fear. "Why, Angelica? Why are you killing the Collingsworth Prize finalists?"

She let the amulet fall to her throat. Her dark eyes flashed. "Are you making a joke, Cousin Dana? The idiotic prize doesn't mean a thing to me. I plan to kill everyone who looted my home. Everyone who broke into the Fear Mansion last year and found my secret room. They took what is mine—and they will all pay for it with their lives."

She petted Candy Shutt's head, smoothing back her red hair.

"I don't understand," I said. "Why did you make it look like *I* was the murderer?"

"To distract everyone," she replied, still petting Candy's head. "To throw suspicion off Jamie so I could do my work."

She moved quickly, spinning away from the poor dead girl's head, and grabbed me by the shoulders. "Enough talk," she said, scowling at me. "You've outlived your usefulness, Cousin dear. And we can't allow you to tell everyone the truth—can we?"

"Wh-what are you doing?" I demanded.

But I didn't need to ask. I knew what she was doing. She was backing me up to the open kiln.

Her fingers tightened around my arms. She pushed me with incredible strength.

"I have a lot more thieves to deal with," she said. "The Night People. They all stole from me, from my house. They all must die."

"Let me go—please!" I begged. "I didn't steal anything! I wasn't around then! Please—stop!"

Gripping my arms, she gave me a hard shove. Back . . . back . . .

I tried to dig my heels in. But my sneakers slid over the concrete floor.

Back . . . back . . .

Her dark eyes glowed with excitement.

I could feel the heat of the kiln burning my back.

"Please—Angelica, please—"

She gave me one last, powerful shove and sent me toppling backward.

30

A wave of burning heat washed over me. As I fell back, toward the open kiln door, I reached out. Reached out with both hands searching for something to grab on to.

My right hand clasped the amulet. As I fell back, I pulled it off Angelica's throat. It clattered to the floor.

I kicked out with my feet. Squirmed away from the kiln. I hit the floor hard on my elbows and knees. My skin burned. I wondered if my clothes would burst into flame.

I saw Angelica bend down to retrieve the pendant.

My one chance. 1 knew I had only a few seconds.

I jumped up. Dove forward. And shoved her with all my might.

The amulet flew from her hand as Angelica sailed into the kiln.

A scream of horror like the howl of a wild animal burst from inside the kiln. I covered my ears, but I couldn't drown out the horrifying sound.

It seemed to go on for hours. An endless, shrill scream of pain.

Orange and red flames rose high, shooting out in all directions. And then, behind the flames, I saw thick swirls of green . . . a green cloud, putrid, so sour-smelling that I had to hold my breath. Choking clouds of green gas, puff after puff, until the garage was filled.

My eyes watered. The odor made me retch.

I gasped as Jamie's body staggered out from the flaming kiln. She stumbled forward, collapsed in a smoldering heap on the floor. And didn't move.

Choking, retching, I dropped onto my knees beside her. Was it Jamie now? Or Angelica?

The howl of pain continued inside the kiln. The green gas spewed out from the open door.

Jamie opened her eyes. She blinked up at me. "Dana? What's going on? Where am I?" She squinted at me. "Hey—what are *you* doing in Shadyside?"

"Jamie?" I cried. "I live with you now. I moved here last month. Don't you remember?"

She sat up. "You live here? Why don't I remember that?"

She doesn't remember anything, I realized. But she seems okay.

From inside the kiln, the screaming came to an abrupt stop. The putrid, green gas slowly faded away.

I've killed her, I thought joyfully. I've destroyed Angelica Fear. She was consumed in the fire.

And then I saw the amulet. Its blue jewels gleamed up at me from the floor. The *real* amulet. Angelica's secret to immortality. The amulet with all its evil magic.

What should I do with it?

I didn't have to think for long. I decided to grab it and toss it into the kiln after Angelica. Let it burn up with her and be gone forever.

I picked the pendant up from the floor and

swung it in the air by the chain. And as I started to swing it into the open kiln door, I heard a fluttering sound at the garage window and saw movement behind me. A darting black shadow.

"Look out!" Jamie cried.

I turned in time to see a huge blackbird come swooping at me. Screeching, it raised its talons.

As it dove toward me, it turned its head, and I saw its missing eye. A dark socket on one side.

I let out a cry as the enormous bird grabbed the amulet from my hand. Grasped it in one gnarled talon. With another screech, it turned in midair. And flapping its wide, papery wings, it swooped out through the open garage window, carrying the amulet with it.

Stunned, I stayed there on my knees on the garage floor. Jamie climbed slowly to her feet. I could see the confusion in her eyes as she grabbed my hands and pulled me up.

"Dana—I don't understand," she started. But then she saw where I was staring, and she stopped.

I was staring at the three heads on the

pedestals, the heads of the murdered girls. Their eyelids began to blink. Their mouths opened. They licked their dry, shriveled lips with purple-black tongues.

And then, as I grabbed Jamie and held on to her in terror, all three heads began to cry out in unison:

"The evil lives! The evil lives!"

TO BE CONTINUED
in FEAR STREET NIGHTS:
DARKEST DAWN

About the Author

R.L. Stine invented the teen horror genre with Fear Street, the bestselling teen horror series of all time. He also changed the face of children's publishing with the mega-successful Goosebumps series, which *Guinness World Records* cites as the Best-Selling Children's Books ever, and went on to become a world-wide multimedia phenomenon. The first two books in his new series Mostly Ghostly, *Who Let the Ghosts Out?* and *Have You Met My Ghoulfriend?* are *New York Times* bestsellers. He's thrilled to be writing for teens again in the brand-new Fear Street Nights books.

R.L. Stine has received numerous awards of recognition, including several Nickelodeon Kids' Choice Awards and Disney Adventures Kids' Choice Awards, and he has been selected by kids as one of their favorite authors in the National Education Association Read Across America. He lives in New York City with his wife, Jane, and their dog, Nadine.

Here's a sneak peek at

FEAR STREET NIGHTS:
DARKEST DAWN

The evil isn't dead yet. . . .

Both girls were screaming now, screaming and crying, and frantically pulling at their hair.

They probably wouldn't make it to the dance.

I decided it was time for me to leave. I raised my wings and took off, floating high above Jamie's house.

They still hadn't seen me. If they had, they would have screamed some more. They would have recognized me, the blackbird with one eye missing.

And they would know that the EVIL lives, the evil still haunts them.

At least, they consider me evil. I have a different point of view. I think I'm on the side of justice. I only want what is fair.

After all, they invaded my house last year. They broke into the Fear Mansion and looted it. They gleefully stole our possessions.

Didn't anyone ever teach these kids that crime doesn't pay?

Well, that's what I plan to do. I plan to teach them that important lesson.

Dana and Jamie think they have killed the evil. Burned it in that fiery kiln in Jamie's garage. They think they can relax now.

But I'm still here.

I'm closer to them than ever.

And I have the amulet. The jeweled pendant that gives me so much power.

They won't get away with their crime. I'll see to that.

I'm not evil. What an ugly word that is. I desire only *justice*.

Trying to burn us away gives me even more reason to seek my revenge.

Even more reason to kill them one by one.

DON'T MISS A SINGLE NIGHT

It all started with Lewis and Jamie. They were sneaking out late at night to be together. Then their friends started joining in. First at the old burnt-down Fear Mansion. Later, at the local bar Nights.

They called themselves the Night People. And they carefully protected their secret world. No parents, no work, no stress. Just chilling with friends in their own private after hours club.

But then the nights turned dark. Unexplainable accidents, evil pranks... and then, later, the killings. The Night People know they have to stop the horror all by themselves, or else they risk exposure. Not to mention their lives.

ISBN 1-416-90412-3